Dear Reader,

I love beginning a new series, and since this is my first trilogy for the Harlequin Romance line, it's doubly special for me. I had so much fun creating the small town of Destiny, Colorado, where families are the foundation, and the roots run deep in the close community.

Tim and Claire Keenan were blessed years ago when three little girls were left in their care. Morgan, Paige and Leah Keenan are the basis for these stories.

The first is Leah's story, *Raising the Rancher's Family*. When photographer Leah Keenan returns home from a tragedy during her travels, she runs headlong into stubborn rancher Holt Rawlins. The sparks fly, but so does the compassion as they help each other heal.

Then next month there's Paige's story, *The Sheriff's Pregnant Wife*. Pregnant and alone, attorney Paige Keenan moves home to raise her baby. Soon her once-boyfriend Sheriff Reed Larkin is hanging around, playing the part of stand-in daddy.

In June Morgan has emotional scars from her past in *A Mother for the Tycoon's Child*. When tycoon Justin Hilliard arrives in Destiny she meets his five-year-old child. In no time the father-daughter duo work their way into Morgan's heart.

I hope you enjoy visiting Town Square, Mick's Dream Mine, Hidden Falls and the Keenan Inn—all the places in my stories that make Destiny so special.

Thanks for reading,

Patricia Thayer

Rocky Mountain BRIDES

Three sisters coming home to wed!

Amongst the breathtaking landscape and tranquil beauty of the Rocky Mountains lies the small, picturesque town of Destiny. It was in this bustling community that the three beautiful Keenan sisters were raised, until college and work scattered them around the globe.

Now Leah, Paige and Morgan are home—finally reunited—and each with a story to tell....

Join the sisters as they each find the one great love that makes their life complete!

This month meet Leah in
Raising the Rancher's Family

In May Paige returns home....
The Sheriff's Pregnant Wife

Look out for Morgan's story in June
A Mother for the Tycoon's Child

PATRICIA THAYER

Raising the Rancher's Family

Rocky Mountain
BRIDES

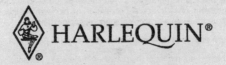

HARLEQUIN®

TORONTO • NEW YORK • LONDON
AMSTERDAM • PARIS • SYDNEY • HAMBURG
STOCKHOLM • ATHENS • TOKYO • MILAN • MADRID
PRAGUE • WARSAW • BUDAPEST • AUCKLAND

ISBN-13: 978-0-373-03943-2
ISBN-10:   0-373-03943-3

RAISING THE RANCHER'S FAMILY

First North American Publication 2007.

Copyright © 2007 by Patricia Wright.

Patricia Thayer has been writing for over twenty years and has published thirty books for the Silhouette and Harlequin Romance® lines. Her books have been nominated for the National Readers' Choice Award, the Book Buyers' Best and a prestigious RITA® Award. In 1997 *Nothing Short of a Miracle* won a *Romantic Times BOOKreviews* Reviewers' Choice Award for Best Special Edition.

Thanks to the understanding men in her life— her husband of over thirty-five years, Steve, and her three grown sons and three grandsons— Pat has been able to fulfill her dream of writing. Besides writing romance, she loves to travel, especially in the West, where she researches her books firsthand. You might find her on a ranch in Texas, or on a train to an old mining town in Colorado, and this year you'll find her on an adventure in Scotland. Just so long as she can share it all with her favorite hero, Steve. She loves to hear from readers. You can write to her at P.O. Box 6251, Anaheim, CA 92816-0251, or check her Web site at www.patriciathayer.com for upcoming books.

To Becky,
I was the new kid in town,
and you gave me a hand and guided me through.
You were there whenever I called for help....
no matter what the hour. Thanks, friend.

CHAPTER ONE

SHE was finally home…

Leah Keenan drew a shaky breath as she drove the narrow road that led up the mountain. To the safe haven of Destiny, Colorado, where she'd grown up surrounded by love and the security of her two sisters and their adoptive parents. It had been twenty-seven years since the day when she, Morgan and Paige had been left at the Keenan Inn.

But she wasn't the same idealistic, fun-loving girl who had left the small town three years ago. The cruelty of the world had managed to change her.

For the past month she'd fought the recurring memories, but with no success. Memories of the Middle East where she'd been photographing the horrors of war for *Our World* magazine. She'd seen so much horror—the bombs, the gunfire, the death and destruction. She just finished filming the earthquake and seen the hundreds of thousands of homeless.

And, oh God, the children…

At the sound of a horn, Leah swerved just in time to miss the oncoming car. Shaken, she pulled her rental car to the side of the road and shut off the engine. In the silence Leah could hear the sound of her pounding heart. She had to get herself together.

After a few minutes, she climbed out and drew in a breath of clean mountain air. She slowly began to relax as she eyed the familiar area. White Aspen trees lined the road, their new growth and rich green leaves promising spring had arrived in southern Colorado. Her gaze rose to the San Juan Mountain Range, the Rocky terrain blanketed by huge pine trees. At the very top were patches of leftover snow from the previous winter.

Leah smiled, suddenly feeling adventurous. As a kid she'd hiked through these foothills as if they were her backyard, and her daring spirit had driven her parents crazy.

Luckily on her flight from Durango she'd worn her standard work clothes—a cotton blouse, pullover sweater, khaki pants and lace-up boots.

Grabbing her trusty camera off the seat, Leah marched to the fence and a sign that read, No Trespassing. Since the landowner, John Rawlins was a friend, she ignored it. She easily climbed over the wire fence, decided the direction she planned to go and set out on the narrow trail.

Leah made her way through the trees toward

the mountainside. A doe appeared in the grove of trees and she paused to snap a picture. The serene beauty of this place helped to soothe her. Eager to reach her destination, she picked up her pace. After another fifty yards, she could hear the sound of water.

In the shade of the trees it grew cool, but she let nothing slow her until she reached the clearing. She stared in awe at the sight and sound of water rushing over the sheer ledge of mountainside into the rocky bottom of the pond below. Years ago, she'd named this special place Hidden Falls. Since adolescence, this had always been her private retreat, her escape where she could daydream.

A sudden movement caught her eye. She glanced toward the base of the falls to find a small child squatting down on a rock and washing in the water. He looked about eight years old, she thought as she snapped a picture of him, then glanced around to look for anyone else in the vicinity. Like a parent.

Not another person in sight.

Leah moved closer and the kid suddenly jerked around and caught sight of her. There was fear in his eyes as he stumbled backward, then regained his footing and took off.

"Hey, wait," she called after him. "I'm not going to hurt you. Are you lost? I have a phone in the car."

The kid didn't stop. He darted through the trees like a mountain lion. Leah followed, but the youngster was too fast. "It's going to get dark soon," she yelled, but the boy was gone.

Okay, he so wasn't going to come to her. Refusing to give up, she continued through the trees as she checked her watch. It was after three o'clock.

"He didn't even have a jacket," she murmured, knowing how cold it would get after nightfall.

Then in the distance she spotted a figure on horseback. As he approached she could see he was a large man with a black Stetson pulled low over his face. Suddenly her attention was drawn to the rifle he held across his saddle horn. She suddenly felt fear, something she'd thought she'd left behind.

"Hello, maybe you can help me," she said a little too breathless. "There's a boy—"

"You're trespassing," he interrupted.

She blinked at his rudeness. "Not really," she said, trying to recognize the man, but his sandy-brown hair and startling green eyes were unfamiliar. "I know the landowner. I'm more worried about the young boy I saw. I think he might be a runaway."

"I haven't seen any kids," he insisted. To her relief, he slipped the rifle back into the sleeve. "So you need to leave."

"I said it was okay, I'm Leah Keenan. John Rawlins has let me hike here to take pictures for years."

"That's not going to be allowed any longer."

Leah wasn't used to people around here being unfriendly. "And why is that?"

"John died about six months ago." She was close enough to see something flash in his eyes, sadness, vulnerability…

Quick tears stung her eyes. "Oh, no, not John. I didn't know." The rancher had been about her father's age. He was also someone she'd loved and enjoyed seeing and talking to.

"Well, now you do." He shifted the big gelding and pinned her with startling green eyes. "So you can leave the property."

"I can't. There's still a lost child. He could be hiding out in one of the caves. That could be dangerous."

"Then I'll ride around and check it out."

His offhanded promise didn't reassure her. "I know where all the caves are around here. I could help you look."

"I don't need your help."

Leah worked hard to hold her temper. "There is no reason to be rude. I'm only worried about the child."

"That child is trespassing, and so are you. Now leave."

Her temper got the best of her and she jammed her hands on her hips. "Just who are you?"

"Holt Rawlins."

Leah's gaze combed over the shadowed face, and finally recognized the strong jaw and the familiar cleft in his chin. The difference was the sandy-colored hair, and those piercing emerald eyes.

"John's son," she whispered. "I didn't know John had a son."

A bitter smile creased his wide mouth. "That makes us even. For years I didn't know I had a father."

Holt Rawlins slowly followed the intruder on horseback and watched as she made her way to the fence and climbed over it. Leah Keenan got into her car and finally drove off.

He breathed a sigh. The last thing he wanted was another resident of Destiny telling him what a wonderful man John Rawlins was. If the man was so great why hadn't he seen or spoken to his only son in nearly thirty years?

Holt's parents' divorce had been a bitter one. For years his mother had told him that his father was a selfish man, that his family hadn't mattered as much to him as his precious Silver R Ranch.

With the notification of his father's death four months ago, Holt had now returned to the place of his birth. To live on the land that rightfully belonged to a Rawlins.

And he was a third generation Rawlins.

He turned the chestnut gelding, Rusty, toward the picturesque waterfall, letting the tranquil sound relax him as he looked through the rows of aspen trees toward the majestic mountain range. Though he was a New Yorker who thrived on the energy of big city life, there was part of him that got a different kind of rush from this place.

He attributed it to the fact that his life was in turmoil right now. He'd ended a long-term relationship with a woman whom he'd thought he wanted to be his wife. His career wasn't the exciting challenge it once had been. So when the lawyer called and said his father had passed away and left him a ranch, Holt knew he needed to come back. At least to learn about the man who was his father. So far, all he'd discovered was that everyone around here had loved and respected the man. His chest tightened. Then why hadn't he had time for his only son?

Holt thought back to the numerous birthdays and Christmases when a small boy had waited for a present, or letter. Just a phone call. But there had been nothing…ever.

He pushed aside the memories and glanced toward the road. All evidence was gone of the petite blonde with the big doe eyes. But something in those deep, chocolate depths told him she didn't give up easily. He doubted he'd seen the last of her, or heard the last praise of a man who to Holt had been no more than a stranger.

Leah drove down two-lane First Street, the main road through town, past the row of buildings that made up the small community of fifteen hundred residents. In the historical town square was the bank, the sheriff's office, City Hall and the mayor's office. Leah smiled. The mayor was her older sister, Morgan.

Leah drove past the large tiered fountain that spouted clear mountain water…for now. Over the years the water mysteriously changed color according to any upcoming holiday.

Not much had changed in the pleasant town she and her sisters had grown up in. That gave her comfort, comfort she needed to help heal her body…and her heart.

She slowed at Pine Street and turned left. Just a block up the road she saw the huge brick and wooden structure she still called home. She pulled up in front of the decorative white sign posted in the yard of the historic bed and breakfast, the Keenan Inn, Tim and Claire Keenan proprietors.

Leah climbed out of the car as her mother rushed out of the house. Right behind her was her father.

"Leah, you're home." Claire Keenan wrapped welcoming arms around her daughter and held on tight. Leah fought her emotions as she inhaled her mother's familiar rose scent.

She kissed Leah's cheek then pulled back to examine her again with concerned blue eyes. "You look tired—and you're too thin."

Leah laughed and brushed away a tear. "Gee, Mom, thanks."

"Step aside, Mother, I need to hold this lass in my arms to make sure she's really my baby girl." Tim Keenan pulled her into a rough embrace and whispered in her ear. "You're home now, Leah, and you're safe. My prayers were answered."

Her father had always had the power to know what she was thinking and feeling. What she needed. The big, burly Irishman had dark good looks with an easy smile and big heart. And from the time Leah had noticed boys, she'd compared everyone to him. Not one of them had ever measured up.

Suddenly Holt Rawlins came to mind again. There was something about the man she hadn't been able to shake. As a trained photographer she'd prided herself on reading people, but not this man.

"Tim, let the poor girl get a breath," Claire said. "Let's go into the kitchen." She took her daughter's hand and squeezed it as she blinked back tears. "It's so good to have you home. You've been away too long."

"I know, Mom."

They walked up the steps to the Victorian house. The large porch was trimmed with baskets of colorful spring flowers. Two wooden swings hung by chains on either side of an oak door with the oval beveled glass inlays. She stepped across the threshold into a wide entry and honey oak hardwood floors. A burgundy carpet runner led to a sideboard that was used as the hotel's front desk. The high white ceilings were trimmed in crown molding. The pocket doors to the parlor were partly closed, but Leah could see two guests sitting at the window enjoying their afternoon tea.

Her mother said something to the girl behind the desk, then escorted Leah past the winding staircase that led to six guest suites upstairs on the second floor.

They passed the library with the fireplace and the big comfortable, overstuffed wing chairs and the shelves loaded with books. Next was the formal dining room with the floral wallpaper and oak wainscoting. Several tables were already set for tomorrow's breakfast with fine china and silver and colorful napkins.

They walked into the kitchen. This room was different from the rest of the house, mainly because it was strictly for family. No guests were allowed in this area. The same went for the Keenans's living quarters on the third floor

Her father led her to the big table in the alcove lined with windows facing the backyard. "Now, tell us about your travels."

As Leah sat down she felt her heart begin to pound, but before she could speak, her mother spoke up. "Tim, leave the child alone. She hasn't even had a chance to catch her breath."

Leah touched his rough hand. "Dad, I want to know about what's been going on here. That Morgan was elected mayor is so cool. I bet that ruffled good old Hutchinson's feathers."

The Hutchinsons had always been the wealthiest family in town. It was their great-grandfather, Will, who first struck it rich with the "Silver Destiny Mine," and had helped found the town.

Claire looked sad. "I think Lyle is more concerned about his father. Billy Hutchinson is failing badly. It's a shame he had to be put in the nursing home."

"I'm sorry to hear that." Billy Hutchinson had to be well over eighty.

Her father stiffened. "Well that didn't stop his son, Lyle, from trying to undermine the election, by strong-arming his employees to vote for him. Lyle wants what's good for himself." Tim nodded. "Morgan will do what's good for the town."

Claire carried a big tureen of potato soup to the table, then filled bowls for everyone. She handed the first one to Leah.

"I have to say, Mom, I've missed your cooking," Leah said.

Claire beamed. "Well, I hope that convinces you to stay longer. Both you and your hotshot lawyer sister."

Leah didn't want to talk about leaving again. She just wanted to think about pleasant things. Like home, and family. "How is Paige? I haven't been able to e-mail her in months."

"She works too hard," her mother said, "but we're hoping to get her home for the celebration."

The familiar voice called out from the hall. "Hey, where is everyone?"

"We're in here." Leah jumped up and went to the doorway as tall, willowy Morgan came in.

Her auburn hair was long and curled around her shoulders. A perfect frame for her green eyes. Morgan and Leah were as opposite as two sisters could be.

"Leah, come here, squirt." Morgan hugged her tight in a comforting embrace. "I'm so glad you're home."

"And I'm glad to be here." Tears prickled Leah's eyes as her sister held her close. So many times while she'd been far away from home, she had relied on her big sister's love and support.

"Come eat, you two, before it gets cold," Claire called.

They walked hand in hand to the table and sat down. After a short blessing, the family began to eat.

"I heard that John Rawlins died," Leah said. "Is that true?"

Her father nodded. "It happened so fast. A heart attack." His gaze met hers. "How did you find out?"

"I stopped by Hidden Falls and ran into a man

who says he's John's son. A Holt Rawlins." She didn't mention that he was good-looking, but not all that friendly. "I didn't know John had a son."

Her father nodded and leaned back in his chair. "Years ago John met his wife, Elizabeth, when she was here on vacation. They fell in love and were married just weeks later. But she never took to being a rancher's wife, and Elizabeth took the boy back East to her family."

"Why didn't Holt ever come here to visit John?"

"John tried, but Elizabeth's family had money and she got full custody of their son. She refused to let him come back here even for a visit."

"Well, he's here now," Leah said.

Her mother sighed. "John left him the Silver R Ranch."

"Is he going to stay?"

"Not sure," her father said. "The word is he's a financial adviser in New York. Why so interested?"

Leah shrugged. "I guess I'm curious as to what kind of man he is," she said honestly. "I noticed a little boy at Hidden Falls. By the looks of him, I'd say he's a runaway. Mr. Rawlins wasn't too eager to help me look for him."

Morgan looked up from her soup. "I haven't gotten a report from the sheriff about any runaways. Are you sure he's not just a camper who strayed? John's property borders the Mountain View Campground."

Leah had seen too many hungry street kids not to be suspicious. "Could be, but tomorrow, I'm going back to look for him whether Rawlins likes it or not."

Her parents exchanged a look. "Maybe you should let the sheriff handle it."

"The sheriff can't do anything if he can't find the child, if he's hiding out. But don't worry, I can handle Holt Rawlins." She thought about the intimidating man with the rifle and hoped that was true.

But she thought wrong.

The next morning, Leah parked her car in the same spot and followed the trail that led toward the falls, but she didn't make it undetected. Mr. Rawlins met her on the trail.

He looked better than a man in a pair of old jeans and a Western shirt that looked like he'd been working for hours had any right to look. He wore his Stetson like a shield, low, concealing a lot of his face.

"I thought I told you I would take care of this," he said.

She raised an eyebrow. "I decided you could use some help," she told him.

He leaned forward, resting his arm on the saddle horn. "You're still trespassing."

"And there's a young boy who could be lost."

"Or he could be running from the law."

"Either way, he's just a child." She folded her arms over her chest. "I'm not leaving."

"I could remove you, or call the sheriff."

"I'll still report seeing a child," she challenged right back. "He'll get a search party together and comb this area."

Holt stiffened. The last thing he wanted was more people coming on the property. Curious residents of Destiny, wondering about his business here.

"Of course with a lot of people searching," she continued, "it could drive the frightened boy into more danger."

"I'll give you two hours. If we don't find anything, the search is over." He held out his hand. "Climb on."

Leah Keenan's big brown eyes rounded. "You want me to ride with you?"

"Since I don't have another mount, and I doubt you can keep up with me on foot, I'd say this is your only option."

She squared her shoulders, bringing her height up to maybe five foot two. He'd always been attracted to tall, leggy women. Of course he couldn't deny he'd noticed her shapely, petite body. At this stage in his celibate life any woman would spark his interest.

"Okay," she relented. "We'll start with the caves."

After his reluctant nod, she marched toward the

horse. He slipped his foot out of the stirrup, and she put her boot in, gripped his forearm, pulling herself up behind him. He had no doubt she was an experienced rider.

"All set?" he inquired.

"I'm set." She grabbed the edge of the cantle on the saddle. "Head toward the hills. I know two caves there. I'm hoping he's holed up in one of them instead of an abandoned mine."

Holt tugged the reins to change Rusty's direction. The transition didn't go smoothly and Leah gasped and grabbed on to Holt to stay on the horse. He tried to ignore the feel of her hands on his waist, but her touch was like a brand burning into his skin. He found he'd missed it once they got on the trail and she released her hold.

"If you need to hold on…"

"I've ridden all my life, I think I can manage to stay on a horse."

About twenty minutes later they finally reached the edge of the rocky hillside. Leah was eager to get off the horse. She was becoming far too aware of the close contact with this man.

"Stop here," she called and dismounted before he could offer to help. She took off up the slight grade of the slope, feeling Holt behind her. She heard him slide in his leather sole boots, but wasn't about to help him. He didn't care about any lost kids. Let him keep up with her. She finally made it to the ledge, and kept going around the rock formation. Years disappeared recalling it had probably been since high school that she'd scaled this rocky terrain.

"Hey, wait up," Holt called to her.

Leah stopped and waited as he came up beside her. For a city guy, he handled the climb like a local. Four months of ranch life had benefited Holt Rawlins in other ways, too. She couldn't help but admire his developed shoulders and chest. Suddenly her breathing became a little rough and she quickly blamed it on the altitude.

"You can wait here if you're claustrophobic," she told him. "The space is kind of narrow."

She couldn't ignore the intensity in his green eyes. "Just lead the way."

She walked around another group of rocks, made it to the other side where there was an entrance to a deep cave. She leaned down to make it through the opening. It was empty and there weren't any traces of it recently being inhabited by a human.

"He's not here," she said disappointed.

Holt sighed and tipped his hat back. "So what's next? Are you ready to give up?"

"No, I'm not giving up," she insisted.

Leah marched out with Holt close behind her, too close. She continued her trek along the wide ledge for about thirty yards. She had hiked this area during her teenage years when she'd first taken up photography.

"How do you know about these caves?" Holt asked.

"I used to come here to take pictures. John told me as long as I stayed away from the old silver mines, he'd let me have the run of the place." She paused and a breeze whipped at her hair as she looked around.

They were surrounded by the brilliant colors of the mountains. Above, a rich blue sky topped each peak, and below, a lush green meadow was spotted with cattle.

"Why did you stop?"

She glanced back at the man. "Just enjoying the view. Your view."

"I don't have time to stand around."

She sighed. *Save me from New Yorkers.* "We're almost there." She went around another group of rocks to the entrance of another cave and she ducked inside the cool space. That's where she saw several empty water bottles. Holt came around her and took his own inventory of empty food wrappers. "It looks like the kid is also a thief."

Leah placed her hand on his arm. "Please, Holt. Your thief, as you call him, is only a boy." She glanced around. "Look how he's had to live."

"He shouldn't be living here."

"Maybe he has nowhere else to go," she insisted. "Have you ever thought about that? He's a child and he's living in a cave." She blinked back sudden tears. "Looks like he has moved on anyway."

For a split second she saw something in his eyes that gave her hope. Holt relented. "I won't have a thief around."

"You won't. I'll come back and find him." She reached into her vest pocket and pulled out two energy bars and placed them on the log. "In case he returns here." She walked out and Holt followed her.

They made their way down to the horse. "What did you mean you'll be back?" he asked.

"The boy isn't going to survive out here for long. The weather could change, and it could freeze. I can't stop looking for him."

"Okay, then come by the ranch and you can have your own mount."

"So, you've changed your mind about the boy?"

"I've only decided it would be safer if he's found."

Well, Leah decided. This man might have a heart after all.

CHAPTER TWO

IN THE bedroom, later that evening, Leah sat on the bed with Morgan, reliving memories of their childhood.

"You'd still be stuck in that tree if I hadn't found you and got you down," her older sister told her.

"It would have been okay if I hadn't got my jeans caught on the branch," Leah recalled. "Mom wasn't happy that I destroyed my new pants."

"That wasn't all she was worried about. It was your lack of fear. And now, you're out there traveling from continent to continent."

"I can take care of myself." At least physically, Leah thought as pictures of forgotten kids flashed into her head. She shook them away. "Mom doesn't need to worry."

"As if she would ever stop," Morgan said. "You're her baby."

Leah had felt secure in the arms of her family. Unlike her sisters, she couldn't remember any life before coming to live in Destiny. She considered the Keenans as her parents. She hadn't been as inquisitive as Morgan and Paige about her biological parents, or why their mother had given up her three young daughters. This was home and now, that meant more to her than she could explain.

"Please tell me you're staying for a while."

"I told you I would be here to help with the town's celebration, and Mom and Dad's anniversary. I don't have to report for my next assignment for six weeks." For the first time since she started photographing third world countries, Leah wasn't eager to return. The constant sight of famine and war had taken its toll on her. Suddenly another picture came to mind. That of the young, thin boy she'd seen at the waterfall.

"What's wrong?" Morgan asked.

"I'm sorry, I'm just worried about the lost boy."

"I can understand," Morgan conceded. "But the sheriff is looking into any reported runaways. Reed Larkin is an ex-FBI agent, and he's good at his job."

Leah wasn't worried about the sheriff. It was Holt Rawlins's attitude that troubled her. "What do you know about Holt Rawlins?"

"Just what Mom and Dad told you." Her sister's green gaze showed concern. "A few months ago he took over the running of the Silver R. He's come into town a few times, but pretty much keeps to himself. Speculation is that he's waiting until after the roundup, then he's going to sell the place."

"Why would a New Yorker spend so much time here?"

Morgan shrugged. "A lot of people want lifestyle changes. Just because you're a globetrotter doesn't mean some of us don't like life in a small town."

"Well, whether he goes or stays, he isn't going to keep me away. I'm headed out there in the morning to continue my search."

"It seems to me you're keeping a pretty close eye on the guy."

Leah stiffened. "Only because Mr. Rawlins seems to have a chip on his shoulder. I don't think he's going to look for the boy."

"So it's Leah to the rescue." Her sister smiled.

Leah only nodded, but knew her track record wasn't that good.

The following morning, Holt came out of the barn to find a compact car pull up at the house. Leah Keenan climbed out and walked toward him. She was dressed in a white blouse, a pullover red sweater and a pair of jeans that molded to that curvy little body of hers. How could someone no bigger than a minute have such long legs?

His gaze moved to her face. Her shiny, wheat-colored hair was pulled back into a ponytail, exposing flawless skin void of any makeup. She walked toward him and her rich brown eyes slowly widened and her full mouth creased in a big smile. Something in his chest tightened when she took off running then he realized her attention wasn't directed at him.

"Zach," she cried as she flew into the arms of the old man standing in the doorway of the barn.

The ranch foreman, Zach Shaw, took her into his arms and hugged her. "Leah," he said. "I heard you came home." He stood back to look at her. "Well, if you aren't still the prettiest girl in town. It's about time you came to see me."

"And if you aren't the biggest fibber ever." She sobered. "I'm so sorry about John. I hope he didn't suffer."

Zach shook his head. "No, it was his heart. He was gone in minutes." The old guy blinked, then smiled. "John talked about you a lot. And he sure enjoyed all the postcards you sent him. He said you'd gone to places whose names he couldn't even pronounce."

"I couldn't pronounce them, either."

They both laughed as Holt watched her wipe stray tears from her eyes and he suddenly felt like the intruder. His own father had known this woman, but never had taken the time to know his own son.

He'd had enough of their friendly chatter. "If you two are finished reminiscing, we need to get started." He walked past them into the barn.

Leah followed. "Just tell me which horse you want me to saddle," she said.

He stopped at the stall. "It's already done."

Zach came up behind them. "I thought you'd do best on Daisy."

Leah patted the mare's neck. "You're a pretty girl," she crooned, then glanced back to Zach. "You didn't have to saddle her."

"I didn't," the old man said. "Holt had her ready before I got the chance."

Holt led his mount toward the door. "I thought it would save us time."

"I'm ready," Leah insisted as she opened the gate, grabbed the reins and followed close behind. "Zach, you want to go with us?"

"No thanks, darlin'." He glanced at Holt. "I'd say this is a two-person job. I'll hold down the fort here. Besides, the little rustler might decide to come back here and steal again."

Leah's gaze shot toward Holt. "Are you sure it was the boy?"

Holt shrugged. "We're short a couple of blankets, a flashlight and some food. What do you think? He came right into the house when we were out with the herd."

"The kid is pretty careful about not being seen," Zach said. "If he's running from someone, that probably means he isn't being treated right."

"And we need to find him," Leah said as she climbed up on Daisy.

"Just be careful, you two," the old man told

them. "Holt, you can handle a horse just fine, but there's a lot in this country you don't know. Leah does. She can lead you to the caves."

Holt nodded. "We should be back in a few hours," he said.

Zach glanced from Holt to Leah and grinned. "Well, if I was a young buck again and had such a pretty companion, I wouldn't be in such a hurry to get back."

Holt grimaced. Damn if the old man wasn't matchmaking.

Leah hadn't realized how much she'd missed riding along a trail in some of the prettiest scenery in the world. She was definitely a mountain girl. She loved everything about the high, jagged peaks that seemed to reach up and touch the sky. Oh, she wished she'd brought her camera.

At least she'd have something to do. She glanced at the man on horseback next to her. Although she'd tried to make polite conversation, Mr. Rawlins wasn't the chatty type. They'd already returned to the cave where they'd found evidence of the boy living there. Everything was gone today. No signs were left of the child.

"Is it just me," Leah began, "or are you like this with everyone?"

He seemed taken aback by her question. "Like what?"

"You haven't said more than a dozen words to me since we left the ranch."

"I didn't think it was required of me to carry on a conversation."

"No, but would it hurt to be cordial?"

He continued to stare ahead. "That all depends on what you want to talk about."

"Well, for starters, why didn't you ever come to visit your father?"

He tensed. "I'm the wrong person to ask that question." He finally turned his green-eyed gaze on her. "I'm sure you or anyone in Destiny knew more about John Rawlins than I did. I haven't seen the man since I was four."

Although Holt Rawlins worked hard to hide it, she caught a flash of sadness in his eyes. And as much as she tried to fight it, his vulnerability got to her. "But John was your father."

"Says you," he said, then guided the horse through a group of trees. "Maybe it would be safer if we concentrated on the task at hand, which seems to be protecting this kid you're so worried about." Even through his gruffness, there was also an undertone of softness in his voice.

"All children need protecting," she said.

"Then, let's find him," he said. "Since he's run off from the cave do you have any idea where he'd go?"

"My biggest fear is that he's holed up in one of

the abandoned mines." She pointed upward toward the foothills.

Holt knew this was a mistake. He should have let the sheriff handle the search for the boy, and then he wouldn't have to deal with Ms. Keenan.

He knew her type. She was out to save the world. Everyone was her friend, and everyone liked her. What wasn't to like? She was beautiful. With her engaging smile that drew you in, it was impossible not to react to her. Those tawny-brown eyes of hers seemed to look too deep…too far inside to see what you didn't want anyone to see.

Yes, he needed to stay far away from the woman. Too bad he hadn't taken his own advice. This morning he'd been up early, waiting and willing to do her bidding.

Holt made a clicking sound with his tongue and the gelding picked up the pace. The sooner they found the kid, the sooner the tempting Leah Keenan would be off his land and out of his life.

About thirty minutes later they reached their destination. Holt followed Leah's lead as she climbed off her mount and tied the bay mare to the tree branch. "The Sunny Days Mine is up there."

Armed with flashlights, she started up the rocky grade with Holt close behind her. To his surprise, she managed to climb with ease. They reached the landing, then another twenty feet they located the mine. The entrance was boarded up and a Keep Out sign nailed across the front. A closer look showed that the barricade had been loosened, making entry easier.

"This is a popular place for teenagers," Leah explained. "It's kind of a rite of passage. They come here to drink and...be with their girlfriends."

Holt pushed back his hat, and rubbed his hand over his unshaven jaw. "This gives Lover's Lane a whole different meaning," he said.

"And it's a whole bunch more dangerous."

He pulled off two loose boards to allow them better access. With flashlights on they ducked into the dark mine. The temperature was a good ten degrees cooler inside and a musty smell assaulted their noses.

Holt directed his light toward the floor, showing dusty evidence of past parties.

"Typical teenagers, they never pick up after themselves," he said.

"We should report this to the sheriff so he can notify the owner to seal the entrance."

"Do you really think that will keep out curious kids?"

Leah ignored Holt's sarcasm. While he examined the main room, she started off toward one of the tunnels, praying she wouldn't find any traces of the boy living here. She ducked through the entry to the tunnel framed by huge wooden support beams. There were old mining tools and stacks of rotten lumber. Just as she walked around the beams, a rat scurried across her path. She gasped and jumped backward tripping over the rotting wood. Unable to regain her balance, she hit the dirt floor as the stack began shifting.

Dust stirred the air and Holt rushed to her side. He swept her up in his arms and carried her out into the main room. Setting her down against the entrance, his large body shielded her from any falling debris. Finally silence filled the air, but he didn't release her. She was trembling, feeling Holt's breath against her ear, his large body against hers.

He looked down at her. "Are you all right?"

She managed to nod.

"Then let's get the hell out of here." He took her hand and drew her outside.

Once in the bright sunlight, he held her at arm's length and did a closer examination. "Do you realize what could have happened to you?"

She was still trembling. "Yes, but I'm okay. Thank you."

That seemed to make him angry. "I don't want your thanks. You could have been seriously hurt or…or…" He turned away, jerked his hat off and combed his hand through his hair. "Dammit, Leah."

Now she was angry with herself. "I know. I shouldn't have gone into the tunnel. I guess I wasn't thinking. I just wanted to find the boy."

"Are you this reckless as a photographer?"

He didn't know the half of it. "They hire me to do my job," she insisted. She started down the slope when he grabbed her wrist and pulled her back. They stood inches apart.

"I'm not taking another step until you promise me not to do anything that crazy again."

The last thing she wanted to do was kowtow to this man, but after he'd rescued her, she owed him one. "Okay, but you need to accept that I mean to find that boy." She glanced up at the sky as the sun suddenly was shadowed by threatening clouds. "We should hurry because we're running out of time." She started down to the horses.

"We're finished for today."

She stopped to argue, but decided it wasn't worth it. "Then I'll go myself."

He gave her an incredulous look. "After what happened in the mine shaft, I'm not letting you out of my sight."

Twenty minutes later they rode back to the ranch, but not before the sky opened up and soaked them before they got into the barn.

The rain pounded against the roof as Leah took Daisy to her stall and began removing her tack. She placed the mare's saddle on the railing, then started wiping down the animal. Once her horse was settled, Leah went to put the saddle away.

"Let me get that," Holt said as he came up behind her.

"I can manage." She glanced at him. He removed his hat and for the first time she got a good look at his handsome face. His sandy-colored hair was wavy and fell against his forehead, and his startling green eyes were framed by long dark lashes. "I…I know where everything goes."

"As do I." He took the saddle from her and continued down the aisle. She went back for the bridle and blanket and hurried to catch up with him in the tack room.

Leah hung it on the wall. "Well…I guess that's it." She turned around to discover Holt watching her. The direction of his heated gaze was on her rain-soaked blouse. At first she resisted the urge to cover herself, but then a clap of thunder shook the barn along with the pounding of the rain. She shivered and crossed her arms over her breasts.

Holt couldn't help but stare. Even soaking wet Leah Keenan was far too appealing. His protective instincts took over and he reached for a blanket. He went to her and draped it around her shoulders. Then he made a big mistake and looked into her big brown eyes. "I think you should wait out the storm here."

"Okay," she whispered. "I'll stay out of your way."

"I have a better idea. Why don't you come up to the house and get out of those wet clothes?"

Her eyes rounded. "I'm fine right here."

"Don't look so frightened, I'm not going to attack you."

She straightened. "I never thought you were. I just didn't want to put you out."

"It's a little late for that," he said as he took her elbow and guided her toward the door. "Come on, the rain has eased up a little."

Together they headed for the house. By the time they reached the porch, they were both soaked again. Holt pushed open the back door and let her inside the mudroom.

"We better take off our boots, or Maria will have our heads for tracking up the kitchen."

"Maria Silva?" Leah looked up from unlacing her boots. "She still works here?"

Holt nodded. "She cleans once a week, and prepares some of the meals."

"Lucky you. She's a great cook."

"I can cook, but after a long day of work, it's been nice not to have to." He went into the main part of the house. He grabbed a towel—and the only thing available for her to change into—one of his flannel shirts. He returned to her.

"I don't own a robe, so this is all I have. While your wet clothes are in the dryer put this on."

"I don't need to change."

"You're shivering. Do it or Zach will kick my butt for letting you catch cold."

"Okay." Leah took the shirt and followed him through the kitchen and down the hall.

He pointed to a closed door. "That's a bathroom." "If you want you can take a hot shower."

Holt climbed the stairs to the second floor of the large ranch house. He definitely didn't need a hot one, he thought as he went into the master bedroom that once belonged to his father. The large sleigh bed was a dark mahogany covered in a multicolored quilt. The small print wallpaper had faded over the years. A braided rug partly covered the hardwood floor that Maria kept polished to a high gloss.

There weren't any pictures of family and none of him, even as a boy. Holt tried to push aside the memories of a man who wanted nothing to do with his son. His only child.

There were three other bedrooms on the second floor, but Holt told himself the reason he stayed in this room was because of the connecting bath. He began stripping off his clothes and heard the water go on downstairs. Great, that was all he needed, the image of a naked Leah Keenan in his bathroom. He got in the shower and turned on the faucet to cold.

But ten minutes later, he went downstairs and found Leah in the kitchen. He swallowed hard. She was dressed only in his shirt. Her face was scrubbed clean and the blond hair pooled wet against her shoulders was beginning to curl.

"Hi," she said. "I hope you don't mind, I fixed some coffee."

She'd made herself at home. "Sounds good," he told her. "I take it you know your way around here."

Leah sipped from her cup. "I'm sorry, it's just that while I was in high school, I used to spend a lot of time here taking pictures."

He tried not to look at her legs, but it was impossible not to, even for a saint and he wasn't anywhere' close to being a saint. Her smooth, shapely calves and trim thighs made his mouth water as the edge of his plaid shirt cut off any more view. He took a gulp of the hot coffee, nearly scalding his throat.

He went to the refrigerator and pulled open the door to the cool air. "How about some lunch?"

She came up beside him, too close and smelling of his soap. "Only if you'll allow me to fix it."

Holt stepped back. "Sure. There are cold cuts in the meat bin. I'll get the bread."

She touched his arm to stop him. "I can do it. Please, Holt, go and sit down."

He nodded, went to the large oval table, pulled out a chair and sat. He couldn't help but watch as she moved efficiently around the kitchen. She laid out the bread on the white-tiled countertop, and layered the cooked ham on top, then added lettuce and tomato. He was handling things just fine until she went to the maple cabinets and reached up for plates. That was when the shirt rose high, exposing the back of her smooth rounded thighs.

Damn. He glanced away. A man could only take so much. Suddenly the back door slammed and in seconds Zach appeared in the kitchen.

The old foreman glanced around the room. His hazel eyes sparkling as he grinned. "Well, if this doesn't look cozy."

CHAPTER THREE

LEAH realized what her being half naked and standing in the Rawlins's kitchen must look like. But she pushed aside her embarrassment, put a smile on her face and went to greet Zach.

"You're just in time for lunch," she announced. "Do you want a ham or a turkey sandwich?"

The foreman glanced at Holt. "I don't want to interrupt…"

"Since when has that ever stopped you?" Holt told him. "You might as well sit down. We're just killing time until Leah's clothes dry."

"So you two got caught in the storm?"

"We were headed back," Leah said. Why was she feeling guilty? "Sure you don't want a sandwich, Zach?"

"Well…if it's not too much trouble." The foreman went to the table and sat down across from Holt.

Leah smiled. "Not for you."

"I take it you didn't have any luck finding the boy," Zach said.

"No, but I'm not giving up," she assured him. "He's out there somewhere." She turned back to her task at the counter.

"I think he's moved on," Holt said. "We haven't seen any sign of him since yesterday morning."

Leah placed the sandwiches on mismatched plates from the cupboard and carried them to the table. "That doesn't mean he isn't out there." She went back and poured two glasses of milk, staying busy to keep calm. "I have some places to check tomorrow." She sat down next to Zach, tugging her makeshift robe over her knees. "I thought I'd try the old Hutchinson mine up on the south ridge."

"That's a thought," Zach said. "There's water close by and even though the cabin is old, it's still in good shape." He bit into his sandwich.

"Hey, don't I have a say in this?" Holt asked. "I can't keep traipsing around the countryside looking for a kid who doesn't want to be found."

Leah tensed. "Then I'll go by myself."

"Not without my permission."

She caught his determined gaze, but she wasn't intimidated. "I'm sure the sheriff could get some volunteers together within an hour and search until nightfall."

Holt glared. "I don't like being threatened."

"Not any more than I like to think about a child

being left out there alone." She got up from the table, went to the mudroom and slammed the door behind her.

"Well, you've done it now," Zach said as he looked at Holt. "Maybe where you come from people don't care about other people, but around here we take care of our own. If you won't go with Leah, then I will."

Holt tensed, knowing it wasn't true that everyone in Destiny took care of, *their own*. His father hadn't. Something tightened in his chest. Even Holt wasn't so callous as to let a kid roam around the wilderness.

"Will you stop grumbling? I didn't say I wouldn't go." Ignoring the gleam in the old man's eyes, he stood and went to the mudroom. He opened the door just in time to see Leah pull her jeans over those long smooth legs.

Damn. His body suddenly stirred to life.

She jerked around and fisted the shirt edges together. "Do you mind?"

Holt leaned against the doorjamb as if the intimacy of watching her didn't bother him at all. Like hell. He forced a smile. "Not at all."

Leah turned her back on him and fastened the jeans. "I'm going back to town now. I'll get your shirt back to you."

"Keep it as long as you want. It looks a lot better on you anyway."

She ignored him and pulled on her boots, then

grabbed her blouse and bra off the dryer. "I'll be back tomorrow."

He nodded. "I'll have the horses saddled about eight."

She froze. "But I thought—"

"I only said I couldn't keep doing this all day…every day. I do have to help Zach with chores, and we're trying to organize the roundup."

"I know." Her expression softened as she came closer. "Holt, I appreciate your time and help, especially after the mishap in the mine."

She looked young…and innocent as she flashed those big brown eyes at him. He felt the reaction deep in his gut. She drew more than protective instincts from him. "That's why you shouldn't go into those mines alone."

Leah nibbled on her lower lip. "So…I guess I'll see you tomorrow morning," she said.

Holt nodded, not trusting himself with saying anything more.

"Goodbye," she said, then darted out the door and down the steps. The rain had slowed to a soft drizzle, but she seemed to hardly notice it. Leah raised her face skyward and drew a deep breath before she got into her car.

From the window he watched her drive off. Had he ever been that carefree? He knew the answer to that. He'd been driven all his life. His mother, Elizabeth Pershing, had expected certain things from her only child. He had to uphold the blue-blood old Boston Pershing family's name. And being the son of a Colorado rancher had already been a black mark against him. As hard as he tried, Holt never felt good enough to be a Pershing. He'd once overheard his grandparents say that Elizabeth had made a mistake marrying, and having a child with John Rawlins. Holt never doubted that he was the "mistake."

The one difference between himself and his mother was he'd finally stopped trying to please the family. When he'd heard of John Rawlins's death—and even with his Grandmother Pershing's threats to disinherit him—Holt had quit his job and moved to Colorado to take over the ranch.

He walked away from his career and from the woman he supposedly loved. Melanie was everything a man could want. But when she wanted to settle down and start a family, he couldn't take that step.

He wasn't sure if he was capable of love.

"Leah, did you hear what I said?" Morgan asked.

"What?" Leah glanced at her sister, embarrassed that she'd been caught daydreaming.

"I asked if you think the church hall is big enough for Mom and Dad's anniversary party."

"Well, you should know better than I do. How many people will the place hold? Are we inviting the entire town?"

The always organized and composed Morgan looked anything but that today. "I'm not sure," she said. "It's just that we've got the town's Founder's Day celebration at the same time."

Morgan was the only one of the Keenan sisters who had stayed in Destiny. Leah had taken off to photograph the world. Paige, with her law degree, took a job with the D.A. in Denver. Morgan's dream had always been to teach school. But while she'd been student teaching in an inner-city school, she'd suddenly come home. To stay. She'd said that she'd changed her mind about her career, then soon after opened a gift shop in the Keenan Inn. Since then Morgan hadn't traveled any farther away from Destiny than Durango. She'd been the one here for the family, especially her sisters.

Leah decided it was about time she and Paige helped out.

"When did you say Paige was coming home?" Leah asked.

"Not sure. The last time I talked to her she was working on a big criminal case. She's hoping she'll make it by the end of the month."

Leah frowned. "That only leaves us two weeks before the party."

"I'll take whatever I can get." Morgan smiled. "I'm just glad you could get so much time off. Three years is too long to be away."

Guilt made Leah blush. "You always knew I was

an eager kid with big dreams. I had to grab an opportunity when it was handed to me."

"Are you sorry?" Morgan asked.

"Of course there are times," Leah began, "that I missed the family." So many nights she'd cried herself to sleep after she photographed all the pain and suffering. It was what hadn't gone into print that truly haunted her. She sighed. "But *Our World* magazine gave me an opportunity I couldn't pass up." For the last three years, she'd led Morgan to think her life was so glamorous, but the faces of the children she had to walk away from would bother her always.

Leah forced aside the memories and smiled. "I wish I'd had better accommodations. Most of the places I went didn't even have running water, or toilets." Or any respect for life.

"Well, we for sure can give you better living quarters. I just hope you don't get bored."

On the contrary, Leah welcomed the peace and quiet of her hometown. Her thoughts turned to Destiny's new resident, Holt Rawlins. He hadn't exactly made her feel peaceful. "I think I can stay busy enough."

"If you're talking about the runaway boy, maybe I should give Reed a call. As sheriff he could get together a lot of volunteers."

"I'm just afraid that we'll drive him deeper into

the woods. Maybe it's better if Holt and I go out tomorrow alone."

"You've been in town for only a few days and you've seen more of our new resident than we have in the past four months." Morgan's eyes widened. "What's he like?"

Leah shrugged. "I see a strong physical resemblance, but he's nothing like John. Has he made friends with anyone in town?"

"Outside of the few times I've seen him at the grocery store or the trading post, he's pretty much kept to himself. He's cordial and polite. Maybe you should invite him to a town meeting and introduce him around."

Leah wasn't sure Holt wanted to make friends. "Doesn't it seem strange that John never mentioned a son?" Leah asked. "Why he never had a relationship with Holt?"

Morgan shrugged. "Could be the divorce was a bitter one, and it's difficult to keep a long-distance father/son relationship going."

Leah drew a breath. "It's still hard for me to imagine John Rawlins ignoring his own child."

"It happens," Morgan told her. "Look at us. Our birth mother never came back to get us."

It was no secret that twenty-seven years ago three girls—two toddlers and an infant—were left at the inn for the childless Keenans to raise. There had never been much discussion about the girls' biological parents. Why would a mother just leave her daughters?

Morgan looked at her sister. "Sometimes parents can't keep their promises."

The next morning, although the sun was shining, the weather was still chilly. It was a perfect day for a ride. Leah brought her camera this time and tucked it away in her saddlebag. She wasn't going to waste this incredible scenery.

Riding Daisy, Leah followed behind Holt on the trail. They'd already checked out two abandoned mines. Only this time, Holt had her stay outside while he looked around. As much as she wanted to protest, she knew better than to push him anymore. So she busied herself taking pictures.

As they headed back they approached the water-fall. Holt reined his horse and turned toward her. He pushed his hat back exposing his handsome face. "How about we take a break?"

"Sure why not."

Leah climbed down and retrieved her camera. She started toward the rushing water, feeling the temperature cool. The fresh mountain air was re-freshing and a fine mist caressed her face as she climbed over the rocky base to find the best angle to shoot a picture. Poised with her camera, Leah was in her own world when she shifted and began to slip. She gasped. Suddenly a pair of strong arms circled her waist and kept her from falling in the water.

Leah regained her footing, then looked up into Holt's green eyes. Her heart raced. "Sorry, I lost my balance."

He gave her a hint of a smile. "Seems that's been happening to you a lot lately."

"I'll try to be more careful." She regained her footing, and climbed onto a big boulder to look around. "That's where I first saw him." She pointed. "At the edge of the pool."

Holt took in the incredible sight of his own piece of Shangri-la. Crystal-clear water sheeted over the granite that protruded from the mountainside. Several large boulders circled the small pond below, its bottom covered by colorful rocks. He heard a clicking sound and glanced back at Leah. She was taking his picture.

"Surely you can find a better subject than me."

"Maybe, but right now you're all I've got." He caught her sly smile. "Just don't turn grumpy on me."

He surprised himself and smiled. "You're pretty sassy for…a kid."

She moved and took another picture. "You need your eyes checked. I'm not a kid."

"There's nothing wrong with my eyesight." He flashed back to yesterday with her in his shirt. Her long legs. "You might be full grown, but in years, you're still a kid."

"And you're so old."

She lowered her camera and he caught a flash of sadness in her eyes. His chest tightened and he wanted to go to her, but decided it wasn't wise to pursue it.

"What do you say we have some lunch? Maria made sandwiches."

He made his way to his horse and returned with a saddlebag and blanket. He found a big flat boulder and spread out the blanket. Leah sat down on the far edge…keeping her distance. Was she really so afraid of him? Maybe she was wise to be afraid.

"Is there anywhere else we should look?" he asked, handing her a wrapped sandwich.

Leah was getting discouraged. Where had the boy gone? She prayed he was safe. "I can't think of where he'd go."

"He must be a pretty bright kid to outsmart adults," Holt said.

She looked him in the eye. "Or he doesn't trust them." She took a bite of her sandwich. "Maybe they've let him down. But surely his parents would put out a missing persons report."

"Not all parents are like yours," he said, looking at her. "Some don't have time for their kids."

Leah saw the pain on his face, the sudden distant look in his eyes that suggested his childhood wasn't ideal. Before she could speak, he moved toward her.

"Don't turn around but your little friend is hiding just behind the falls."

Leah gasped as Holt's arms encircled her shoulders. "I'm going to try to get a better look, so go along."

She nodded. "Okay, but don't frighten him off."

Holt smiled. "Then you better help." His head lowered as his arms went around her back and drew her closer. She tried not to react, but he radiated heat, and there was the feel of his muscular chest. When he nuzzled her neck she had to fight her response.

"The little thief is moving closer to the edge of the water."

Holt shifted so his mouth was close to her ear. She could feel his warm breath, the brush of his lips as he spoke. Agonizingly sensitive to even such a slight touch of his mouth, the delicate outer curve of her ear seemed to tingle and burn.

"You were right, he's only about eight or nine, dirty blond hair."

"That's him," she whispered. "How are we going to convince him we're here to help?"

His lips moved to her cheek, then her jawline. She shivered as an ache started in her chest and began to shift lower. She didn't need this complication. A man like Holt wasn't good for her. "Is this a good idea?"

He raised his head just inches and stared down at her. "I'm not sure...you tell me." Just then his mouth closed over hers.

Leah was totally lost in the kiss as Holt drew her closer against his body. Wrapping her arms around his neck, she forgot everything but the feel of Holt's mouth against hers. Then slowly he lifted his head, breaking the intimate contact. He sucked in a shaky breath as his eyes drifted open and locked with hers, revealing the heat in the emerald depths.

Suddenly he blinked and turned his attention over her shoulder. "Damn. He's gone."

Before Leah could clear her head, Holt took off after the kid. She scrambled to her feet and hurried along the edge of the pond behind Holt. There was no sign of the boy.

"We lost him."

"I thought you were watching him," she said accusingly, hating that she let this man affect her.

He combed his fingers through his hair. "I was until you decided to be a participant in the kiss."

"Me? You're blaming me for distracting you? It was your idea."

He came up to her, displaying the heat in his eyes. "Yes, and it was a really bad idea."

Holt was silent all the way back to the ranch. Fine. Leah wasn't taking the blame for losing sight of the boy. And she was still blaming herself for losing herself in the kiss, no matter how incredible. But just because there were sparks didn't mean they should do anything about it.

Outside the barn, they dismounted. "Okay, now I have to call the sheriff," she told him.

"Go ahead, but I'm telling you that kid doesn't want to be found," Holt argued.

"Then we're going to have to persuade him we want to help him." She tugged on the reins and led her horse into the barn. Once in the stall, she began to unfasten the cinch straps, then she lifted the saddle off and put it away in the tack room. They'd had three days, and hadn't been able to find one young boy. It was time she called the sheriff.

After putting everything away, she returned to the stall. That was when she saw Zach and Holt at the other end of the aisle and went to tell them of her plans.

Holt took her by the arm. "We need to go up to the house and talk." He started to walk, pulling her along with him.

Leah resisted. "What do we need to talk about?"

His eyes narrowed. "Things."

This time Zach joined in. "Yeah, things."

Leah allowed the two men to lead her outside and up to the house. Once in the kitchen, she swung around.

"You're not going to talk me out of calling the sheriff. We can't find the boy on our own, and it's going to be pretty cold tonight."

"He's living in the barn," Holt said calmly.

"You're kidding." She could believe their good luck. "Really?"

Zach nodded. "I had to go up to the loft earlier. I found a blanket, some clothes and a stash of food."

"That kid has been stealing things right from the house," Holt said accusingly.

"He's trying to survive the only way he can," she pleaded, wondering if this man actually had a heart.

"Well, he can't do it in my barn."

Leah shook with anger. "Of course not. That would be too much trouble for you. That child needs help and you're only worried that he's taken a few of your precious things. I bet you didn't even miss them."

Holt glared. "You know I'm getting tired of being the bad guy. I just meant that a barn is no place for a kid to live. Go ahead, call the sheriff and tell him to come out here." He walked out, letting the back door slam shut.

She looked at Zach. "What's he going to do?"

"Nothing as bad as what you're thinking. He's probably going to find the boy."

"Great," she grumbled and had started after him when the phone rang.

Zach answered it and called her back. "It's your sister."

Leah took the receiver. "Hello, Morgan."

"Leah, the sheriff is on his way out. There's a report of a missing boy from Durango. The boy that fits your description is Corey Haynes. He ran away from his foster home."

"He's been hiding in Holt's barn, in the loft. I've got to go."

Leah hung up and ran for the door. "His name is Corey," she called to Zach.

Running down the steps, she saw Holt with Corey in tow. His hand was around the boy's skinny arm, pulling him toward the house. His clothes were filthy, shirt and jeans were torn, and his white tennis shoes nearly black. The child cursed as he resisted their forward progress.

Leah ran to meet them. "Corey, it's okay. You're safe now," she told him.

He continued to fight Holt. "Just let me go and I'll leave."

Holt finally managed to get the kid into the kitchen. Pulling out a chair, he parked him there, but he jumped up. Holt pushed him back down, feeling the tender spots on his shins, knowing he'd probably have bruises tomorrow.

"Sit down, or I'll tie you down."

Fear filled the kid's blue eyes, but also defiance. Then surprising Holt, he sat down. Holt grabbed another chair, swung it around and straddled it in front of the boy. "Okay, kid, I need a name and where you came from."

"I'm not going to tell you shi—nothin'." Head bent, he stared at the kitchen floor.

"Is it Corey?" Leah asked. "Corey Haynes?"

The boy looked at her and blinked those innocent blue eyes at her. "I don't know any Corey."

Leah squatted down beside the boy. "Corey, you don't have to be afraid. We're here to help you."

"Yeah, I heard that before," he muttered. "Just let me go."

"No way," Holt said. "You can't live in caves."

"Why not? It was a lot better than where I was." Tears flooded his eyes and he swiped them away.

Leah gave Holt a pleading look. He could see she'd already lost her heart to this kid. "Were you mistreated?" She touched the boy's arm and he didn't pull away.

"What difference does it make? Nobody cares."

"I care, Corey," she insisted. "I want to help you."

He looked up and his dirty face was streaked with tears. "Why?"

"Because you deserve better than you're getting." She moved in closer and pulled the child into an embrace. Her nurturing touch seemed as natural as her next breath. "No child should have to live in a cave, or a barn. You should feel safe and secure. And clean." She wrinkled her nose. "You don't exactly smell too great."

She rose and looked again at Holt. "He needs a shower. Is it okay?"

How could he deny her? "Sure…why not."

"How about I take him?" Zach said.

"Will you go with Zach, Corey?"

The boy hesitated. "Will you be here when I get back?"

Smiling, she brushed his shaggy hair off his forehead. "Yes. Just scrub from head to toe."

"I'll make sure he does," Zach said as he led the boy down the hall and into the bath.

Leah turned toward Holt. "Oh, I never thought to ask, do you have anything Corey can wear?"

"Zach will come up with something."

The last thing Holt wanted to do was get involved with this kid's problems. But from the moment he'd found Leah on his property, she'd managed to draw him into her search. He'd followed her around, looking in every cave and mine shaft for a kid who didn't want to be found. He'd gotten far more involved with her than was good for him, especially after the kiss. Not one of his best ideas.

"You think just because he gets cleaned up that's going to make things better?" he told her.

"It's a start," she said, folding her arms over her chest stubbornly. "And I'm not going to abandon him."

"Looks like you might not have a choice," he said. "The kid's a runaway. And once the sheriff gets here he'll have to go back to his foster home."

"The kid's name is Corey Haynes. And he'll never go back to an abusive home. Not if I have anything to say about it."

"You don't know anything about his situation. And you won't have anything to say about whether or not he goes back."

She stood there and stared at him. "What in your life has made you so bitter?"

He didn't need her snooping into his private life. "Not everyone has had a life as secure and charmed as the Keenan girls."

Leah started to speak when there was a knock at the back door. Holt went to answer it.

"Hello, I'm Sheriff Reed Larkin," the man standing outside said.

Holt shook his hand. "Holt Rawlins."

"I knew your father," the sheriff said. "Sorry for your loss."

Holt responded with a nod, and motioned for the man to come inside to the kitchen where Leah was waiting.

"Hi, Reed."

"Hello, Leah. Looks like you've been busy since you got home."

Leah caught the good-looking sheriff's grin. Tall and muscular, Reed had nearly black hair and dark brown eyes and he'd always been crazy about her sister Paige.

"You know me, Reed, I get bored easily."

"You still should have called me to let me know about the boy." He pulled out his notepad along with a grainy picture. "This is the runaway, Corey Haynes, age eight."

"That's him," Leah agreed. "But we can't send him back to his foster home. The boy has been gone nearly a week. Why didn't the foster parents report him missing until today?"

Reed nodded. "They're being investigated, so the boy has a reprieve…for now. But he'll have to go to a shelter for a few nights."

"No," Leah said, her gaze darted back and forth between the two men. "I promised Corey that I wouldn't let you take him back."

"Leah, there isn't much else I can do," Reed said. "His mother is deceased and his father's in jail on a robbery charge. There's no one. And foster homes are overcrowded."

"He'll just run away again," Leah said.

The sheriff was about to argue when his radio went off. "Excuse me, I need to take this." Reed stepped onto the porch.

Holt watched as Leah paced nervously. He knew from the beginning how involved she'd gotten in the boy. He told himself that he'd done his duty by finding the kid. That there was a nice foster home that would care for him. But seeing the frightened look on the boy's face, he knew that wasn't true.

They both turned to the sheriff when he came back in the door. "Sorry, that was Social Services…they were letting me know that there are no foster homes available. So that means I have to take him to Durango to a group home."

"No, you can't," Leah cried. "Maybe my parents will let Corey stay—"

"He can stay here…" Holt interrupted her. "We'll give it a try anyway."

Leah's gaze darted to Holt. "Here?"

"No offence, Mr. Rawlins," the sheriff began, "but I don't know you. And if I were to recommend you for temporary foster care say for the next few days, I'd need more—"

"I know him," Leah jumped in. "We've spent the last three days together searching for Corey. And…Zach's here, too. He'll be around."

Holt watched as Reed contemplated the suggestion. "And Leah will be staying here, too," he added.

"You sure about this?" Reed Larkin asked.

Leah tried to hide her surprise at Holt's suggestion. She would do anything to keep the boy safe…even live under the same roof with this man. "It's time Corey started believing in someone," she said. "Besides, until we find a suitable home for the child, this is the best solution."

Reed looked at Holt. "I'll get in touch with Social Services and they'll be contacting you." The sheriff paused. "Are you sure this is what you want?"

Leah held her breath waiting for the answer.

"I'm sure," Holt said.

"They'll probably send someone out to your house."

"That's fine. I have nothing to hide."

Just then Corey came into the kitchen. He was scrubbed clean. His hair was two shades lighter, and he was wearing an oversize white T-shirt that hung past his knees with a pair of socks on his feet. The boy's smile disappeared when he saw the man in uniform.

Leah went to him. "It's okay, Corey. This is Sheriff Reed. He's going to let you stay here with Holt for a few days. Is that okay with you?"

Corey looked at her. "Will you be here, too?"

"Sure, for as long as you and Holt need me."

CHAPTER FOUR

LEAH rolled over in bed and opened her eyes to sunshine coming through the window. She wasn't in her bedroom at the inn. Sitting up, she glanced around the space and slowly began to remember.

She was in the guest room at the Silver R Ranch. In an old iron-framed bed covered in a wedding ring quilt, and wearing one of Holt's white T-shirts. The panicked look on Corey's face had prevented her from leaving last night, not even for the short time it would have taken to get some clean clothes. At least she'd called her family and told them about the situation.

Leah pushed back the covers and got up. She retrieved her jeans from the chair in the corner, pulled them on, along with her blouse and stepped into her boots.

After brushing her hair Leah walked down the hall of the big, old ranch house. Obviously the place had been neglected for years, but there was beauty hidden under the faded wallpaper and worn carpet. The hallway led into four bedrooms, and a bathroom and the master suite at the far end.

At the top of the curved staircase, she held on to the oak banister and started down the wide steps covered in a dark brown runner. At the landing, halfway down she faced the entry at the front of the house and the solid oak door that had weathered over the years. She descended the remaining steps, thinking this place would make a wonderful home.

She headed for the kitchen in search of the new owner. In the doorway she stopped to see Holt Rawlins standing at the old stove, a towel tucked in the waist of his faded jeans. He wore a chambray shirt and scuffed boots.

She smiled. If only she had her camera.

A sullen Corey was busy setting the table and neither one were talking. Disappointed, she'd hoped that some sort of bonding would take place between the two. Obviously that was going to take a little more time. So as not to disturb them she was about to return to the bedroom when Corey looked in her direction.

"Leah," the boy called. "You're awake."

Upbeat, she walked into the kitchen. "I sure am. I smelled breakfast and couldn't wait to eat." She looked at Holt. "What do you need me to do?"

"Nothing," Holt said. "I have everything under control. There's coffee in the pot."

Even in his own home, he was a man of few

words, she conceded. She went to the coffeemaker. Once she doctored her brew, she took a long sip. "It's good."

Holt continued cracking eggs into the skillet. "How can you tell? You add so much cream and sugar."

"Not so much. It's just most men make it so strong."

He gave her a sideways glance. "I'm not most men."

True, she'd never met anyone like him. Someone who was so stubborn, brooding…handsome.

"How did you sleep?" he asked.

"Not too bad."

Their gazes locked, and Leah's heart began to race. She doubted it had anything to do with the caffeine. "So, how long have you been up?" she asked.

"Since five-thirty."

"You should have got me up. I could have helped with the chores."

"We finished them fast," Holt assured her.

"You and Zach?"

"And Corey."

The boy walked to the cupboard and took down plates. "Holt woke me up to help feed the horses."

She set her mug on the counter. "Well, on a ranch there are chores that have to be done. Animals have to be cared for."

"That's what Zach said," Corey told her as he carried the plates to the table. "Do you know that Lulu is going to have a foal in a few weeks?"

"I remember Lulu," Leah said, recalling John's favorite mare. "A pretty chestnut." A loaf of bread was on the counter. She took out four slices and dropped them in the toaster.

"Zach said that if I'm here I can watch the foal being born. He said it'll be Holt's first time, too, because he never lived on a ranch until four months ago. He came from New York." The boy took a breath and went to get the flatware. "Have you ever been to New York?"

Leah glanced at Holt and saw him in a whole new light. So the man was trying. "Yes, I have, Corey. It's a big place," she answered.

"I only lived in Texas and Colorado. My dad used to work in the mines until they shut down." The boy's expression grew sad. "He couldn't get a job after that and we had to move a lot."

Before Leah could comfort him the back door opened and Zach walked in. "Hey, looks like I'm right on time."

Corey went to him. "Breakfast is almost ready, Zach. After we eat can I go with you and Holt to feed the herd?"

The older man frowned. "That all depends. We still have to finish some chores around here."

"I can help, too." The boy's eyes lit up. "I'm a

good worker. I made my bed and cleaned up the bathroom like Holt asked."

"That's good, because everyone around here has to carry their weight." Zach poked the boy in the stomach and made him laugh. "First, we need to eat so you can put some meat on your skinny bones."

"Breakfast is ready," Holt called as he carried a platter of eggs and bacon to the table.

Leah buttered the toast, then took her contribution and set the plate down next to a jar of jelly. After the food was distributed, Corey asked if she was going to come with them.

"I need to go into town this morning." She caught a sad look from Corey. "Just to pick up some clothes. Don't worry, I'll be back in a few hours. In fact, I'll fix dinner tonight."

"Promise?" the boy asked.

The panic on Corey's face caused her pain. If she could help it, she'd never break another promise to a child again.

"That poor boy," Claire Keenan said as she sat across from Leah at the inn's kitchen. It was probably the first time her mother had been off her feet in hours.

"So I didn't feel I had a choice. I have to stay at the ranch."

"First thing this morning, I called Esther Perkins at the church. She's rounding up some clothes for the boy."

"Thanks, Mom. I'm also going to stop by the trading post and get him some underwear and socks—and a pair of shoes. He has a pair of old tennis shoes that I don't think even fit him." She thought about Corey's former foster family and got angry all over again.

"I know you've wanted to help this child, Leah, but I'm concerned about you, too. You've gotten so involved in the situation… Are you going to be all right when he goes to a foster home?"

Leah wasn't ready to talk about her own demons. She only knew that she couldn't walk away from this boy… Not like she had before with another child in another place, another time.

"It's Holt Rawlins who's taken the responsibility for Corey. I'm just helping him out."

"You've moved out to the ranch. I'd say you were helping quite a bit."

"Mom, how can you talk when years ago you and Dad took us in."

Claire Keenan smiled, tiny lines crinkling around her beautiful eyes. "Outside of marrying your father, it was the best day of my life. And from the moment we saw you, we fell in love with you, Morgan and Paige."

Leah grasped her mother's hand across the table. "And I love you and Dad. But please try to understand that since I'm the one who found Corey I do feel responsible." She blinked back tears. "It sounds crazy, but it's as if I were meant to help him."

"And he's lucky to have you," her mother continued. "I'm just concerned about what happens when you have to leave for your next photography assignment."

Leah didn't want to think about that. "I'd never hurt Corey intentionally."

"I know, but a lot of people deserted him in the past."

She groaned. "I have six weeks off. Maybe he'll be in a good foster home by then."

"Or maybe Holt Rawlins will keep the boy with him."

Leah frowned. "Well, they were getting along better this morning." But Holt as a foster parent? That was too much to expect. "I assume Holt will be going back to New York."

"That's not what I heard."

They both turned as Morgan walked into the kitchen.

Dressed in a far too long and loose fitting dress, her sister seemed determined to play down her beauty. She came to the table. "Mr. Rawlins has taken the Silver R Ranch off the market," she told them.

"Holt Rawlins is going to stay and run the ranch?"

Morgan shrugged. "That's what Susan Horan told me this morning. She's the real estate agent who was handling the property."

Leah had thought that Holt's plan was to go back to New York…and his life there. She wondered if there was someone special in his life. Her thoughts took her back to what happened at the waterfall yesterday. How could there be another woman when Holt had kissed her like he had?

"So tell me, little sister, you're home less than a week and you've already managed to move in with the best-looking man in town."

She frowned. "Morgan, you know why I stayed at the ranch last night. Because a frightened little boy needed me."

"I know." She raised her hand. "But you have to admit Holt Rawlins is a good-looking cowboy."

"Cowboy? Holt Rawlins is from the East."

Morgan's eyebrows rose. "Then let's agree he's got a lot of his father in him. The man could be on a billboard. Just ask any woman in town."

No one had to tell that to Leah. She could still see his smile, feel his touch and taste his kiss.

"Of course the town council was hoping to get a section of the Rawlins property," Morgan said.

"Why?"

"We're interested in promoting more tourism for revenue. A new ski area and hiking trails are at the top of the list. The Silver R's property cuts off access to what we have. I approached John about it, but we never really got down to the details before he passed away." She smiled at Leah. "Since you know Holt better than anyone else in town, I thought maybe you could talk to him."

"Oh, no." Leah jumped up. "The man barely tolerates me. And I don't know him that well"

"Sure. That's why he asked you to move in and help him with a runaway boy?"

"No, because Sheriff Larkin was threatening to take Corey to a group home." Leah paced. The one thing she did know about Holt was he was leery of people, especially of his father's friends. "Give me a few days to see how things go with Corey. Then I'll introduce you to Holt and you can ask him." She checked her watch. "I need to go shopping for a young man."

Leah spotted the apple pies cooling on the counter. "Hey, Mom, you wouldn't have any extra, would you?"

"Oh, I think your father can get by with one pie."

Pie in hand, Leah kissed her mother and sister goodbye and took off to do her errands. The first stop was the trading post to pick out clothes for Corey. She couldn't help but wonder how long it had been since the boy had anything but hand-me-downs. Well, a new pair of jeans and a shirt was a must. She walked by the shoe section and spotted a pair of buckskin boots.

She smiled. Every cowboy needs his own pair of boots.

* * *

Leah arrived back at the Silver R Ranch about two o'clock in the afternoon. When she found the house deserted, she went down to the barn. No one was there, either. It wasn't until she heard voices that she wandered outside to the corral where Corey sat on top of Daisy and was being led by Zach around the arena.

Holt sat on the fence as Corey took instructions on riding. Leah took the time to watch the man on the railing. As much as he tried to act indifferent, she could see he was intensely interested in the boy's progress.

Why did Holt hold himself so apart? What had happened between John and Holt to keep a father away from his son? She had a dozen questions that she knew she wouldn't get answered anytime soon. So she focused on the happy looking boy on the horse. Maybe Corey would be the one who broke through the man's tough shell.

One could always hope.

Suddenly Holt's face went through a transformation. His mouth twitched and curved into a hint of a smile.

The sound of Corey's laughter made her turn to the small rider on the horse. Zach had let go of the bridle so the boy handled the reins on his own. The youngster beamed as he sat high in the saddle and directed the horse around the corral.

"You're doing great, son," Zach called.

Leah watched as Corey glanced toward Holt. Even she could see that the boy wanted his approval.

She strolled to the fence, climbed onto the railing and sat down next to Holt. "Corey's doing great."

"Zach's been working with him." Holt turned to her. "Did you bring your things?"

"Yes," she told him. "Enough for a few days. I also picked up some clothes for Corey."

"The sheriff stopped by about an hour ago. He dropped off what the boy had at the foster home. Just some old clothes and another pair of worn tennis shoes, barely enough to fit into a grocery sack. I almost tossed it in the trash. But Corey grabbed the bag and took it into his bedroom as if it were some sort of treasure." He sighed and tipped his hat back.

"Oh, Holt. That's so sad."

"Yeah, and it doesn't get any better. Seems Corey's dad is in prison, and he isn't eligible for parole for a long time."

Her heart ached. "So he's been in foster homes for a while."

He nodded. "Speaking of which, Reed also said we'd be getting a visit from Social Services. Probably tomorrow." His gaze met hers. "I want you there with me."

Leah felt the heat from his look, trying to tell

herself this was only for the boy's sake. "Of course. And I want to thank you for doing this for Corey."

"It's temporary, Leah. I can't offer the boy any more."

She wanted to argue the point, but saw the pain in Holt's eyes. There were so many things she wanted to know about this man. But she knew he wasn't willing to share. Maybe he never would.

It was after seven o'clock. Leah had just finished cleaning the kitchen after supper. Zach retired to his small house out beyond the barn to watch television. Holt had disappeared into the den to do some paperwork. What did she expect from the man, to keep her company?

Corey came barreling into the kitchen dressed in his new blue Western shirt, dark denim jeans and a pair of buckskin boots. "Leah, how do they look?"

She smiled at his excitement. "You look great. How do the boots fit?" She knelt down on one knee for a closer look.

"I put on two pair of socks like you said." He nodded. "So they're okay."

She stood. Corey had eagerly accepted everything her mother had collected from the church. "Well, you'll probably outgrow them in a few months."

"I can wear the other pair of boots you brought when I help Zach tomorrow."

"Good idea. They're already broken in." The

ladies at the church had been generous in sending clothes along with a pair of kid's boots.

Just then Holt walked in. He glanced at Corey then continued to the coffeemaker. After pouring himself a cup he turned around and leaned against the counter. He eyed the boy more closely. "You need to break those in."

"I will," Corey said and glanced at Leah. "Maybe I should wear old jeans to work in and save these for good."

"If that's what you want," she said.

Holt gestured toward the clock. "It's not too late if you want to watch some television before turning in."

Corey nodded, then paused before leaving to look back at the two. "Good night, Leah. Thank you for the clothes."

"You're welcome. And good night, Corey."

The two males exchanged a nod and Corey disappeared from the kitchen.

Leah turned back to Holt. He was watching her. "Coffee?"

"No, thank you." She had enough things to keep her awake without the help of caffeine. "I think I'll say good-night, too."

Holt didn't want Leah to go yet. He'd spent too many nights alone in this house. He was beginning to doubt his decision to stay. "Wait," he called to her. "We need to talk about tomorrow."

She raised an eyebrow. "What's up tomorrow?"

"The social worker. She's coming out to see if I'm providing a suitable temporary home for Corey."

"Well, are you?" she challenged.

"You seemed to think so about twenty-four hours ago. Are you having second thoughts?"

"No. It's just that I'm worried about Corey. He seems a little jumpy around you."

"I've hardly said anything to the kid." He put down his cup and came to her. "And he avoids me about as much as you do."

Her eyes widened. "I told you I had errands to run and clothes to pick up."

"So you're going to be around tomorrow?"

"Of course. I want Corey to stay here—at least until they find a good permanent home for him."

Most likely that wasn't going to happen. Not many people wanted to adopt an eight-year-old boy. "That'll be a problem for the future. But if Corey is to live here for the time being, we need to play the happy couple…for the social worker."

"We didn't tell Reed we were a…couple."

Holt shrugged, enjoying her discomfort. "I'm not sure what we need, but when Social Services shows up we should at least act like we know each other."

"I guess you're right." She turned those velvet-brown eyes on him. "So, give me a rundown on yourself in twenty-five words or less."

That made him smile. She made him smile. "So,

don't you want to know more?" He cocked an eyebrow. "What if I have a sordid past?"

"What if I do?" she returned. "I mean, I've been out of the country for the past three years."

His eyes roamed over her petite frame that he'd come to appreciate more and more. Leah Keenan looked like the all-American girl. Just the type you took home to the family—the type you married. Definitely not his type.

"Were you ever in prison? Have you taken illegal drugs? Robbed a bank?"

"Of course not. You can contact the magazine I work for in New York. They'll vouch for me."

He fought to hold back a grin. "I was kidding. You've got small-town girl written all over your face"

"Unlike the city slicker from New York."

Holt had no doubt that she'd heard about his childhood when he'd lived here. "You already know John Rawlins was my father. When my parents divorced, my mother took me back to her family. I stayed there until college, and afterward I worked as a financial adviser for a Wall Street firm. I'm not married, not engaged, there isn't even anyone in my life…at the moment."

She drew a breath. "I lived here in Destiny since I was four months old. Since the day my mother brought her three daughters to the Keenan Inn and left us."

"Whoa…" He frowned. "How did that happen? How could she…?"

She shrugged. "I'm not sure how she could have done it. According to my adoptive mother, our biological mother didn't have a choice. Claire and Tim Keenan adopted us as soon as legally possible. So you see that was the reason I couldn't leave Corey to fend for himself."

Holt was surprised by her story, but Leah lived in a fantasy world. "There may not be a damn thing we can do to help Corey."

CHAPTER FIVE

IT WAS nerve-racking for Leah.

They were all gathered around the kitchen table as the social worker from Durango, Lillian Gerard, wrote in her notebook. She'd talked with Corey earlier, getting his personal account of his life in the last foster home.

"I'm not going back," Corey told her. "You can't make me."

The middle-aged woman stopped what she was doing and turned her attention to the boy. "We're not going to make you go back, Corey. We've discovered things about the...situation that make the house you were in unsuitable. The question now is, finding you another place to live."

"I want to stay here."

Mrs. Gerard looked at Holt. "That's what Mr. Rawlins and I have to discuss."

Holt straightened in his chair. "Corey, why don't you take Lulu an apple," he said.

Leah knew the boy loved to feed the mare. But he hesitated before he got up, grabbed the fruit from the bowl on the counter and headed out the door.

"Okay, Mrs. Gerard, let's cut to the chase," Holt began. "Do you have a home for Corey?"

She sighed. "Honestly, no. There's nothing available at the moment. He'll have to go into a group home."

"No, he can't," Leah said angrily. "He's only eight years old, and in the last two years, he's been in four homes. He's run away from every one of them."

The social worker looked sympathetic. "I know, but there just aren't enough good foster homes available."

"Isn't there's a relative who can take him?" Leah inquired, hoping they'd searched for someone who would care. She turned to Holt for support, but he sat stone-faced.

Mrs. Gerard looked over the file once again. "There is a distant cousin but she's in poor health. And since Corey's been labeled hard to handle, the available foster parents passed on him."

"Well, look how he's had to live," Leah said defensively.

"There's another option," Mrs. Gerard said. "He could stay here…temporarily."

Holt raised an eyebrow. "I qualify as a foster parent?"

"Since your home meets all the requirements, I

can give you emergency status, thanks to Sheriff Larkin's recommendation of you and Miss Keenan…and I know Leah's mother." She smiled. "And of course, we had to do background checks on you both. But most importantly, I've seen how Corey is when he's around you." She sighed. "So the question is, Mr. Rawlins, are you willing to keep the child here in your home?"

This time Holt's gaze connected with Leah's. Even though he'd been gruff to her, he'd been fair to the boy. He would be the perfect guardian for Corey.

"I'm a bachelor, Mrs. Gerard, I'm not sure I know how to parent…."

"None of us know how to be a parent in the beginning, Mr. Rawlins. We more or less learn as we go. I've seen you interact with the boy. He respects you. That's a big step."

Holt turned to Leah. "Are you going to hang around?"

She found she'd been holding her breath. "If you need me to, I'll be here." Was she crazy? How could she cohabit with this man?

"All right, Mrs. Gerard, I'm willing to keep Corey here…until a suitable home is found for him."

Over the next twenty minutes Holt filled out paperwork and they finally said goodbye to the social worker and watched her drive away.

Holt looked at Leah. "What have you gotten me into?"

PATRICIA THAYER   83

"Me? I was willing to take Corey to my parents' home. You stepped in and said he could stay here with you."

His mouth quirked. "Well, you're in this with me." He stepped closer. "So pack your bags, darlin', because you're moving in. Looks like we're going to be one big happy family."

Later that afternoon, Holt adjusted his hat as he walked to the barn. He'd been crazy to let Leah talk him into this. But he'd let her talk him into a lot of things. The fact of the matter was, he'd let her get to him. New York had been full of beautiful, sophisticated women who knew the score. He'd been able to pick and choose and pretty much call the shots. But the one time he'd tried to have a long-term relationship, he'd failed miserably.

Now, it seemed the tables had been turned. Sassy Leah Keenan was calling the shots and suddenly he was responsible for an eight-year-old boy.

How could he give guidance to a child when he'd lacked positive male influences in his own life? Hell, his own father hadn't been in his life for years. Even his maternal grandfather hadn't been attentive to him as a child, or as an adult. His chest tightened as he recalled the familiar rejection. No matter what he'd achieved in sports, academics, in his career, Holt never could live up to his grandfather, Mackenzie Pershing's, expectations. And he'd never been given the chance to live up to John Rawlins's.

Holt entered the barn and found Zach cleaning a stall.

"So how did it go?" the old man asked.

"Looks like the kid will be around for a while," Holt told him. "I'm going to take out Rusty."

The old man beamed. "That's a good idea. Why don't you ask the youngin' to go along?"

Holt headed to the tack room. "Not now, I need some time alone. Besides, he and Leah are deciding how to fix up his room." He took the saddle off the sawhorse and carried it to the stall.

Zach followed after him. "You want to know what I think?"

"Not really." Holt soothed the gelding and slipped the bridle on.

The foreman ignored him. "Since you arrived here, you've kept to yourself too much. There's some good folks around here. Being a little neighborly wouldn't hurt."

"I'm a New Yorker. We're not known for being overly friendly."

Zach removed his worn hat and scratched his nearly bald head. "Just like your father. For years after your mother took you away, John pretty much stayed here, avoiding people." The old man smiled. "Until little Leah showed up. She was in high school back then, and cute as a button. All legs, and with braces on her teeth. She was going to be a photographer and she wanted to take pictures of Hidden Falls. Said it was for a school project. John wasn't too keen on it at first, but she was a pesky thing and finally he gave in. That boyfriend of hers kept bringing her out here…"

"Her boyfriend?"

"Yeah, some big football player. I think they call them jocks now. Whoever he was, he followed her around, doing her bidding."

Holt didn't want to hear about Leah's old boyfriends. "I know the feeling," he murmured as he spread the blanket over the horse's back.

"You say something?" Zach asked.

"No." He lifted the saddle onto Rusty's back and began to tighten the cinch.

"Well, like I was sayin', Leah was a frequent visitor out here. John got so he looked forward to seeing her."

Holt was tired of hearing about Leah's happy times with John Rawlins. "I'm going to check the herd. I'll probably finish repairing the pasture fence and be back in a few hours." He slipped on his gloves with the hope that some physical work would help kill his awareness of Leah.

"You know, Holt, you're turning into quite the rancher. You haven't shied away from any of the hard work. Your father would be proud."

"Too bad it took so long for me to get back here."

The old man rubbed his jaw. "Maybe there were things John couldn't control. I wish you could have known him."

Holt stiffened. "And that's my fault? The man knew where I lived. He chose not to see me."

Holt led Rusty out of the stall hoping to find some peace. He sure wasn't going to get much with a full house.

That next afternoon, Leah went looking for the absent Holt. With directions from Zach, she rode Daisy along the fence into the grassy valley. Since Mrs. Gerard left yesterday she hadn't had a chance to talk with Holt. Alone. She had a suspicion he was avoiding her. Well, he wasn't going to ignore her any longer.

She spotted Rusty tied to a tree and not far away was the man she'd been looking for. She rode closer and discovered that he'd removed his shirt, leaving him in an undershirt, revealing his muscular shoulders and arms. Sweat beaded against his skin as he worked to stretch barbed wire along the newly placed post.

Holt looked up as she approached. He didn't seem happy to see her. "Is there a problem?"

"No, Corey's fine," she said as she climbed off her mount. "He's with Zach."

Holt went back to stretching the wire. "Then why did you track me down?"

"Maybe if you didn't just disappear all the time, I wouldn't have to. We need to talk."

He finished hammering the horseshoe nail into the wood, then turned to her. "Okay, tell me what's so important that it couldn't wait until I got back?"

"I wanted to talk to you…" She was suddenly distracted by the sweat glistening on his shoulders. "I mean about…how we handle Corey. Since it's summertime he doesn't have school. And he has a lot of time on his hands."

"Well, I don't," Holt told her. "I have a ranch to run. Next week is roundup. Tomorrow we're bringing the herd here."

"That's what I meant, if you would have taken the time to tell me…"

Anger flashed in his eyes as he dropped his hammer. Pulling off his gloves, he walked toward her. "And why would I feel the need to do that?" Under the shade of the trees, he removed his hat and stopped in front of her. "You're my pretend wife, Leah, not my real one."

"Nor would I want to be," she retorted.

His gaze roamed over her body making her feel exposed. Then he smiled. "Don't knock it, if you haven't tried it." He reached out and touched her cheek. "Maybe we should practice at being loving parents."

Leah pushed his hand away. "Stop it." She stepped back. "What is wrong with you? I thought you were okay with having Corey live at your house."

"I am. He's not a bad kid. It's you I'm having trouble dealing with."

She was hurt. "Me? But you asked me to move in. In fact you insisted on it."

Holt shut his eyes momentarily. He had insisted, but he didn't realize the toll her living in his house would take on him, on his sanity. "Yes, but all day every day. You're everywhere." If she wasn't in the kitchen, cooking, he could hear her laughter throughout the house. Even when he walked by the bathroom, he could catch the scent of her soap. His gaze locked with hers. "You're too tempting, Leah."

Her face reddened. "I'm not trying to be."

"But it's the reality."

"But for Corey's sake, it wouldn't be a good idea to act on those thoughts."

"So it's for the kid's sake that you rode all this way?"

He watched her breathing grow rapid. She gave him a weak nod.

"You're a liar, Leah" he accused. "You could have waited until I got back. Maybe you're feeling it, too. This thing between us."

Against his better judgment, he took a step closer.

She couldn't get away because Daisy was behind her.

"I should get back."

He knew she was right. He knew that he should just send her away, but ever since that day at the falls when he'd kissed her, he'd wanted to kiss her again.

"You should have just left me alone, Leah. A man can only take so much." He never realized how overwhelming just knowing she was sleeping down the hall from him… She was the first person he saw in the morning and the last person at night…

If he let her, she could become an obsession. "You want me to say that I want you? All right, I do."

His mouth lowered to hers, his lips caressed hers, then he pulled back to see her blink her big eyes at him. He was barely holding on to his control. "Tell me to stop, Leah, and I will."

She just stared at him, then parted her lips as he dipped his head toward hers. When his mouth closed over hers, she whimpered and placed her arms around his neck and let her lips part so he could deepen the kiss. He did. He tasted her and it was intoxicating. He wanted more. Much more. His arms wrapped around her and pulled her against his aching body. He was drowning in her, and never wanted to come up for air.

Finally his common sense prevailed, and he broke off the kiss. He gasped for a breath and stepped back. Was he crazy?

"Go back to the house, Leah," he demanded as he turned away.

Leah stood there frozen to the spot. She'd been crazy to let Holt kiss her. Crazy to get involved with this man. She had to stay focused on a more important problem. "Holt."

"I said leave, Leah."

"You can't keep ignoring Corey."

He turned around and nodded in agreement. "I'm not that big a bastard. I know I shouldn't ignore him. It's just that some of us aren't the best role models."

"It's not as hard as you think, Holt. Just give him some of your time, a little attention. The boy hangs on to your every word. I've already seen him emulate your mannerisms."

"I don't want him to," he told her. "His stay isn't meant to be permanent. Corey will be leaving."

"Well, while he's here, he's chosen you to be his hero."

The following evening, Holt drove into town and parked the truck in front of the Keenan Inn. Leah's parents had invited all of them to dinner. It was great for Corey and Leah, but he wasn't sure he was ready to socialize, to play out their situation in public. And he'd learned that Tim Keenan had been a good friend of John Rawlins.

"Wow! Your house is so big," Corey said from the back seat of the truck.

"Remember I told you that we only live on the third floor. The rest of the house is for guests," Leah explained. "Come on, Mom and Dad are waiting."

Corey eagerly climbed out of the truck's back door. He was wearing the new clothes that Leah had bought him. His hair, although still long, was neatly combed off his forehead. For all his excitement, the boy moved behind Leah when her parents come out on the porch.

Holt knew the feeling. He found himself putting his hand on the boy's shoulder as Leah hurried up the steps to embrace her family.

"It's okay, Corey. The Keenans are nice people."

The boy still looked frightened. "What if they don't like me?"

Holt couldn't help but smile as he pulled off his Stetson. It was funny how quickly boots and cowboy hats had become his uniform. "Just be polite and remember what we talked about."

"I know, mind your manners."

It was Mrs. Keenan who came down the steps and smiled at the boy. "My, what a handsome, young man. You must be Corey."

"Yes, ma'am," he said. "It's nice to meet you, Mrs. Keenan." With a nudge from Holt, he reached out his hand.

She shook it. "It's nice to meet you, Corey. And all the kids call me Mrs. K." She raised her gaze to Holt. "You must be Holt Rawlins. It's so nice to finally meet you."

"Yes, ma'am." He shook her hand as Leah's father showed up.

"Hello, Holt. It's nice to see you again." The older man smiled.

"Thank you for inviting us, Mr. Keenan," Holt said.

"It's Tim and Claire. And lately, it's the only way we can see our daughter," Tim joked. "But what she's doing is more important. Right, lad?"

The boy nodded. "Nice to meet you, Mr. K."

A younger woman arrived on the porch. She was a good four inches taller than Leah and had long auburn hair. Holt recognized her as Destiny's mayor. "Corey and Holt, this is our oldest daughter, Morgan," Mrs. Keenan said.

"You're the mayor," Corey said.

The pretty woman smiled. "Yes, I am. You can call me Morgan."

"And it's great to have two more guys to even the odds at the dinner table," Tim said. "Maybe we can talk sports for a change. How do you feel about the Denver Broncos?"

Holt had been a New York Giant fan all his life. "I'm looking forward to the upcoming season," he told his host as they went into the house.

As they walked through the house into the warm, aromatic kitchen, Tim Keenan said, "You both are in for a treat. My Claire is the best cook around."

Holt smiled. "I've been looking forward to sampling it all day."

Leah watched as Corey stayed close to Holt. Seeing his protective hand on the boy's shoulder something tightened around her heart. Since her trip out to the pasture, Holt had spent more time with the boy. At first it was awkward, but the two were making strides. At least they'd fared better than she at trying to forget Holt's kiss.

"Everything is ready," her mother called. "Holt, Corey and Leah, sit over there." The big table was set for six. A large pot roast, bowls of vegetables and a basket of homemade rolls were placed in the center.

When they were all seated, the blessing was said and food passed out. The conversation was lively while eating the scrumptious supper. By the time they'd finished dessert, everyone was relaxed. Her father took Corey up to the attic to search for some toys and games to take back to the ranch.

They were finishing coffee when Morgan directed her attention to Holt. "From what I hear, you've settled into ranch life."

"I have to admit it's a lot of work, but yes, thanks to Zach Shaw, I'm getting the hang of ranching." He smiled. "Of course, I might change my mind after the roundup next week."

Morgan turned to her sister. "Didn't you help John with the roundup a few times?"

Leah glanced at Holt. "A long time ago. I was just a kid."

"Don't let her fool you, Holt. She was quite the cowgirl back then."

Holt studied Leah. "Oh, really. You never stop amazing me."

"Well, don't expect much. I pretty much followed John's and Zach's lead." She glared at her sister.

"Do you have other men to help out, Holt?" her mother asked.

"Zach has lined up some of the neighbors, Jim Bakersfield and Bart Young."

"Good, men," Claire said. "It's nice that you're going to meet some of the townspeople…since you're going to be living here."

The mayor raised an eyebrow. "Isn't it mighty peculiar you being a New Yorker that you've decided you want to live here?"

"I was born here," he said. "It wasn't my choice to leave." He glanced around the room. "I'm sure everyone in town knows about my parents' marriage. At the moment, I'm where I want to be— here in Colorado."

Morgan smiled. "And we're glad to have you."

Tim appeared in the kitchen doorway. "And your father would be happy that you're running the Silver R. It was something he'd planned since the day you were born."

Holt stiffened, trying to hold on to his reserve. He'd never known what his father wanted…only that he hadn't wanted him.

CHAPTER SIX

MUCH later that night, unable to sleep, Leah sat at the kitchen table. She had her laptop open and decided she needed to go over the series of pictures she'd taken on her last assignment. Her editor had e-mailed a list of the pictures they wanted to use for the magazine's next issue.

If there was any consolation to her job it was that a lot of readers would see the famine and destruction in the already war-torn area. She wanted her photos to help the cause, the children especially. Another picture appeared on the screen and Leah stopped breathing.

Soraya. She was a beautiful little girl. At the age of six, she'd already experienced too much heartbreak in her short life. She had lost her entire family in the earthquake and had been living in a tent camp, begging for food from anyone who would throw her some scraps. When Leah found the child she was starved and close to death.

Leah clicked the mouse and another picture appeared. Soraya's big brown eyes looked back at her. Leah clicked on another, and another as tears rolled down her cheeks.

"What are you still doing up?"

Leah recognized Holt's voice. She swiped the tears from her cheeks and looked up to see the bare-chested man standing in the doorway, dressed in only a pair of low-riding jeans. She swallowed hard. "I couldn't sleep so I decided to do some work. Sorry, I didn't mean to disturb you."

He shrugged. "I heard you come downstairs, but when you didn't return, I wanted to see if you were okay."

"Just a little keyed up." She didn't want to talk about herself. "Corey had a good time tonight."

"Yeah, he did." Holt walked to the table. "What about you? You look like someone stole your puppy."

She forced a smile. "I was just concentrating on work."

Holt knew it was a lie. She'd been crying, and he hated the fact that it bothered him. That he felt the need to comfort her. "What have you got there?"

"Some of the pictures I took on my last overseas shoot."

"Mind if I have a look?" He didn't wait for her permission and looked over her shoulder.

She hesitated. "I…I guess not. This group is from my most recent assignment. I was shooting the thousands of people who are still displaced by the earthquake." She began to scroll through the pictures.

"Man, these are something." He studied each picture and was amazed at how Leah had captured the defeat and despair on their faces. Next were the children with their hopeful smiles as they posed for her. It was hard to look at their emaciated bodies, realizing they were caused by starvation. A beautiful dark-haired girl appeared on the screen whose big dark eyes tugged at his heart.

"They needed so little, but yet, so much," Leah said, tears in her voice. "And with all the other tragedies in the world, there just isn't enough money, enough help. No child should have to live this way." Along with the sadness came an angry tone. "It's all so cruel…so tragic."

Holt pulled up a chair, sat down and placed an arm around her. "I know, but you can't save them all."

Leah covered her face with her hands. "But why couldn't I have saved one?" she asked. "Just one little girl, Soraya." A sob racked her body. "Oh, Holt, she was doing so well… I found her a shelter, and I promised to come back to see her. I was going to bring her home to the States so she could live with me."

She shook her head as tears flooded her eyes. "I couldn't save her. She died."

Holt drew her into his arms and held her close

as she cried. He wanted to absorb some of her pain, her agony. How long had she carried this with her? "It's not your fault, Leah. It was a natural disaster in a country devastated by years of war."

She raised her head and looked at him. "But I promised her I'd help her…to keep her safe."

Now her obsession with Corey became clear to him. "Leah…you did the best you could do. You were probably the only one who took the time for Soraya. For a short time, you were able to give her love…and hope."

That seemed to make her pause. "You think so?"

Emotions tore at him as he nodded.

As if she all at once became aware of their closeness, she sat up straight. "My editor needs me to go back."

Seeing the pictures, Holt suddenly realized how dangerous her job could be. The last thing he wanted was for her to go back.

"I thought you had at least a month."

"I do. But they never really want you to take that much time. I'm staying until after Mom and Dad's anniversary."

He found he didn't want her to leave at all. "I'm not an expert, but I think you could use some time off."

"But the more pictures I take, the more the world will see what's going on there…with the children."

"So, single-handedly you're going to try to save them all?"

"No, but I need to do something."

"And your pictures do that. People will see these children in the magazine." An idea hit him. "Do these photos go to your editor?"

"They've already bought the ones they want. These others are mine."

Mesmerized, he studied the photos again. "I hope you know, Leah, you're an incredible photographer." Her pictures should be displayed in a gallery, or at the very least put into a book, he thought.

Leah gave him a trembling smile. "Thank you."

"I'm just speaking the truth," he told her, thinking about his friend, Jason Mitchell, back in New York. He owned a gallery on Fifth Avenue and specialized in new talent.

Although he would be getting more deeply involved in her life, he couldn't seem to stop himself. Suddenly he realized he'd do about anything to keep her safe…and here. And it had nothing to do with the deal they made about Corey.

The next morning, Holt got up at dawn, but there weren't any sounds from Leah's room as he passed by. Corey was already in the kitchen and starting breakfast. Holt had to admit that the boy was a hard worker.

"Mornin', Holt. Zach said you and him are going to move the herd today. I was wondering, since I cleaned my room, if I could go with you?

Holt knew how hard the boy had worked the past week to learn to ride. And he'd done pretty well. Holt also remembered all the times he'd wanted to go places with his grandfather, but the man seldom had time for him. Zach was right, a boy needed to prove himself.

"It's going to be a long morning. You sure you're up for it?"

Corey's eyes widened in expectation. The freckles across his nose and cheeks seemed to become more prominent. "Zach said I can handle it. He's been teaching me to rope and cut a calf from his mama."

"I guess there's no better teacher than Zach. He's been doing it for a long time. He even taught me."

"I know." Corey took a pitcher of orange juice from the refrigerator. "Zach said you turned out to be a pretty good cowboy, too—for a city boy."

"He did, did he? That's high praise. Well, if he thinks you're ready, then I suppose you are."

Those blue eyes rounded. "Really? I can go?"

Holt nodded.

The boy let out a loud whoop. But before Holt could quiet him down, Leah appeared in the doorway, her hair mussed, her dark bedroom eyes still heavy from sleep. Dressed in a conservative pink cotton robe, with a print gown underneath, she exposed just enough of her leg to cause his blood to race.

"What's going on in here?" she asked.

"Sorry, we didn't mean to wake you," Holt said.

Corey went running to her. "Leah, Holt says I can go to help move the herd today."

"That's great," she said, then looked at Holt and smiled. "Guess that makes you an official ranch hand then."

"I've got to get my boots and my hat." The boy ran out of the room.

Leah smiled tentatively at Holt. She'd tried to stay in bed until he had left the house. She was still vulnerable from their middle of the night encounter. He'd learned more about her than her own family. What amazed her was he just let her talk and cry it out. And the sexy cowboy hadn't taken advantage of the situation. He was so not the man she once thought he was. Why did he try so hard to hide this side of himself?

Leah marched across the room and stood in front of him. "Looks like you're playing hero again."

"It's not my intention," he said uncomfortably. "But it's not going to hurt Corey to come along."

"Well, whatever, you've made a little boy pretty happy. And thank you for helping me out last night, too." She rose up on her toes, wrapped her arms around his neck and pulled his head down to meet hers.

The minute their lips met Leah knew she was in trouble. She quickly discovered she wasn't in control of anything, least of all her heart.

* * *

The woman made him crazy.

Holt looked across the herd of Herefords to see Leah riding along with Zach. The old man was right. She knew how to handle a horse. And Corey had wanted her to come with them, too.

Ordinarily he wouldn't mind having her ride with them, until she'd planted that kiss on him this morning. A kiss so explosive he nearly lost all coherent thoughts. Then she ended it and walked out the door as easy as you please.

Well, he wasn't going to get involved. She had nice girl written all over her. A woman who didn't play games. She was the worse kind, a woman who wanted a permanent relationship. But he hadn't been willing to do a lot of things until Leah Keenan came barreling into his life.

Zach walked his horse up beside him. "How you holdin' up?"

"I'm fine. Why?"

"You keep looking in my direction." A lazy grin spread across his weathered face. "Of course maybe it wasn't me you've been lookin' at. Could it be Leah?"

Did the old man have radar? "It's my land, I can look anywhere I please."

"If it helps ease your pain, she's been stealing glances at you, too. The boy and her make a nice pair."

Holt sighed. "You're the only pain I have. Now, why don't you help me get this herd into the pen?"

Zach rode off, his laughter ringing in Holt's ears. Damn. The last thing he needed was to think about Leah all the time. He had enough on his plate with the ranch, and Corey. He didn't want to fall for a woman who was going to be headed off to God knew what country.

He'd always been the one to walk away first. That way it didn't hurt so much. Who was he kidding? He'd had a lot of hurt in his life. It hurt that his own mother couldn't see past the hatred she had for his father and love her son. He hated that his own father couldn't love him enough to come and see him.

He looked up as Leah kicked Daisy's flanks, sending the horse into a gallop as she went after a stray. Her hair was flying in the wind, her body moved in unison with the animal. They moved as one, and he thought he'd never seen anything more graceful. Corey cheered her on as she chased down the calf and directed it back into the herd. Suddenly Leah's attention turned to Holt and she smiled.

Or anyone more beautiful.

"This was the best day ever," Corey said as they returned to the barn.

Zach walked by carrying his saddle. "You may not say that later when your backside is aching."

"My backside doesn't hurt."

"Just give it time," Leah said, starting to feel the effects of four hours in the saddle. "But you're right,

Corey, it was fun. It's been a long time since I've ridden like that."

"It was so cool when you went off to get the calf."

"Well, when you're older, you can do the same thing. I've had a lot of practice. Maybe…" She paused not knowing how long he'd be here. "Maybe Zach can teach you."

"Or Holt can," the foreman said. "He can handle a cow pony pretty good. I'd say he was a fast learner."

The boy's eyes rounded. "Really?"

"Well, I already knew how to ride before I came to Colorado," Holt said. "I just had to adjust to a Western saddle."

Zach closed the stall gate. "Yeah, Holt used to wear those fancy breeches and hat, and use a funny looking saddle."

"That's because it was an English saddle." He frowned at the foreman. "We don't chase a lot of cows back in New York."

Zach's eyes twinkled. "Just a funny wooden ball."

"Polo. You played polo?" Leah asked. She couldn't hide her surprise as her gaze roamed over the ultimate looking cowboy.

Holt glared at Zach. "I did for a few years. My grandfather belonged to a polo club. It was a tradition. Do you have a problem with that?"

Leah shook her head. This man never ceased to

amaze her. Even knowing it was dangerous to her heart, she found she wanted to know more about him.

"Holt, will you teach me to play polo?" Corey asked.

"I think we're a little busy now," Holt told him.

"Maybe you have some pictures?"

"Not that I brought with me." He turned away. "Maybe we should think about finishing the morning's chores."

"Maybe we should have lunch first," Leah suggested. "It's after twelve."

"Okay, I'm getting pretty hungry," Zach said. "What do ya say, Corey, that we head up to the house and put together some sandwiches?"

"I'm hungry, too," the boy said.

"I'll heat up the soup my mother sent out yesterday," Leah called after the two as they headed toward the barn door. "Give me a few minutes."

Leah finished with Daisy and walked out of the stall. She was about to take the saddle and bridle back to the tack room when Holt stopped her.

"I'll get it," he told her. "You go on to the house."

"Are you coming?"

"I have things to do," he said. "I'll be by later."

She'd seen him withdraw when he'd started discussing his life back east. "You know," she began, "there are a lot of things in our past we'd all like to forget. Things we can't change. My big concern right now is making a life for a little boy. And he needs you to help him."

"I've given him a roof over his head."

"And that's wonderful. But you of all people should know that's not the only thing that's important. He needs you."

His eyes met hers. She saw stubbornness in the green depths, but also a vulnerability that reminded her of Corey.

"If you want some sort of family man, you better look somewhere else. That's something I can't give him."

She wanted to pound some sense into this man, but at the same time she wanted to pull him in her arms and let him know someone cared about him.

"You might be surprised, and in the meantime you might just find what you've been looking for, too." She turned and walked away so she wouldn't do something stupid again.

Like kiss some sense into him.

That night, Holt rolled over in bed and glanced at the clock. It was nearly midnight. He cursed as he threw back the sheet and sat up. It had been nearly a week since he'd been able to sleep. Hell, he hadn't had a decent night's sleep since Leah Keenan stormed into his life.

He couldn't stop thinking about her, the kisses

they'd shared, her softness…the feel of her body against his. The ache he'd felt whenever she was close.

Damn. He raked a hand through his hair. He was slowly going crazy. He got up and went to the window, opening it wider in search of the mountain breeze. Anything to cool off his heated skin. He got some relief, but not enough. Nothing could drive Leah from his thoughts…from his already complicated life. The strange thing was, he didn't want her to leave the ranch. She'd filled the old house with energy and laughter. Even as he'd tried to stay in the background, she'd pulled him in, including him in a family she'd help create with Corey.

Holt shut his eyes. As a kid, he'd wanted to belong, but every time he'd reached out to his grandfather, he'd been rejected. And he never had a chance with his father…

The stillness was suddenly interrupted by a soft cry. He immediately recognized Leah's voice coming from her room next door. He grabbed his jeans off the chair, pulled them on and went out into the hall. He listened at her door and heard the pain-filled sound again. After a moment's hesitation he let himself into the dark room. With the aid of the moonlight through the window, he saw her slender body thrashing around on the bed and went to her.

"Leah. Leah, wake up." He sat down on the mattress and gripped her shoulders. "Leah, wake up."

She finally gasped and jerked upright. "Holt?"

"You were having a nightmare."

Leah brushed the hair from her face and drew in a deep breath. "I'm sorry. I didn't mean to wake you."

"You didn't. I'm more concerned about you. Are you all right?"

She nodded, but the moonlight revealed the fear in her eyes.

"Do you have nightmares often?" he asked.

"Sometimes," she said, her gaze avoiding his. "Really, Holt, I'm okay."

He knew she wasn't. "Maybe you should talk to someone…professionally."

"I'm fine. It's just, sometimes the memories…"

"You're not fine, Leah," he said. "You've spent a lot of time in war-torn counties. You were probably dodging bullets in your dreams." That thought made him shiver. "At the very least, talk to your family."

"It's not that bad. I just need to get some rest. I'll be fine by the time I go back."

He tensed. She was leaving. "So you're continuing your quest to save the world."

"I have to. I made a promise…" A sob shook her slight frame.

He wrapped his arms around her. "Shh, it's all right," he whispered. "I'm here." He brushed a kiss against her hair as he held her. "Oh, Leah. What am I going to do with you?"

She burrowed into his embrace. "Just…don't leave me."

Never, he promised silently. "I won't." Impulsively he bent down and placed a kiss on her mouth before pulling away. "Just let me check on Corey." He hurried down the hall to the boy's room and found him sleeping soundly. After covering Corey with a light blanket, he returned to Leah. Holt closed the door behind him and went to the bed. Her wide-eyed gaze showed her sudden apprehension.

"Holt…maybe it would be better if you go back to your room."

He sat down and picked up her trembling hand. "Do you really want me to?"

She hesitated, then shook her head.

"Then go to sleep, Leah." He stretched out on top of the blanket beside her, and pulled her close. "I'm right here…if you need me."

"Thank you," she whispered as she curled against him, her hand resting on his chest. Within seconds she was sound asleep. It took Holt a lot longer, but having Leah close was worth a sleepless night. For the first time in a long time, he didn't feel alone.

The next evening, Leah was anxious to see her sister, the mayor, in action at the town council meeting. She had also managed to convince Holt to attend. Since he was staying in Destiny, he should get to know the town's residents.

That had been all she'd managed to talk to him about during the past day. Even though they'd shared a bed most of the previous night, he hadn't said a word about it.

That morning, she woke up when she felt him brush a tender kiss against her forehead before he left her bed at dawn.

Maybe it was best they hadn't discussed sharing the moment together. They had already gone too far beyond the reason for them being together.

Corey.

The small community of Destiny was already talking about their situation. Maybe it was time Leah thought about moving back to her parents? Corey would understand.

"Are you sure there are going to be other kids here tonight?" Corey asked as Holt pulled his truck into the parking space.

"There usually are during the summer," Leah told him. "My parents and Morgan will be there. And there's always cake and cookies."

They climbed out of the truck and walked together toward the old hall. The structure held maybe three hundred people and served many of the town's functions. On a warm night like tonight, it was bound to be filled. Everyone was gearing up for Destiny's Founder's Day celebration. And Leah suspected that they wanted to meet their newest citizens, Holt Rawlins and Corey Haynes.

At the door, her father waited. "Hi, Dad."

"Leah." Tim Keenan greeted her with a kiss. "Corey, good to see you."

The boy smiled as her father ruffled his hair. "Hi, Mr. K."

Tim Keenan looked at Holt. "Holt, nice to see you could make it."

The two shook hands. "Your daughter can be pretty persuasive."

Tim winked. "She gets that from her mother."

Claire Keenan appeared. "I heard that." She offered her daughter a kiss and one for Corey. She surprised Holt and hugged him. "Holt, it's nice you're here."

He glanced around. "It looks like a big turnout."

"It is," her mother said. "And a perfect opportunity for Tim to introduce you around." She nudged her husband and the two men walked off together. "And, Corey, there's someone I want you to meet." Claire glanced around then motioned at someone. Suddenly a dark-haired boy about eight years old appeared.

"Corey, this is Mason Langston. Mason, Corey Haynes. Mason, Corey is staying at the Rawlins Ranch. He hasn't had much of a chance to meet anyone. Do you think you could show him around?"

"Sure, Mrs. K." He looked at Corey. "Hey, do you like chocolate chip cookies?"

Corey shrugged. "Yeah."

The boy motioned to follow him. "Come on, before Kenny Dorsey eats them all."

Leah watched the two boys run off.

"Not to worry, they'll be fine," Claire told her.

"I know, but Corey's very vulnerable. He's been through a lot."

"And Mason is a good boy. He'll be nice to Corey." Her mother turned her attention to her husband and Holt as they made their way around the hall. "The two older boys seem to be getting along nicely, too."

Leah was glad that Holt was meeting people. "Holt should know his neighbors," Leah said. "He's going to live here."

"He seems to be attracting the ladies, too."

As much as Leah tried to ignore that comment, she noticed that Kaley Jenkins Sims was standing very close to him. "Kaley hasn't changed since high school. She goes after any good-looking male. I heard she's divorced now."

"About a year ago," her mother said. "She has a sweet little girl."

Leah found she didn't like seeing Holt and Kaley together. "Well, it looks like she's on the hunt for number two."

"Maybe you should stake your claim," her mother suggested.

That got Leah's attention. "What? I'm not going to stake any claim. I'm committed to my job. Besides, the man has a lot of baggage. The last thing Holt wants is a woman in his life."

Claire Keenan smiled. "You can always change your career. And all men claim to be loners before they realize they can't live without us. From what I can see Holt Rawlins is interested in you."

Leah couldn't consider that possibility. She had a feeling, whether intentionally or not, the man could hurt her.

Holt looked up from the conversation and glanced across the hall at Leah. He knew she was enjoying this. He'd met so many people tonight he'd never be able to remember their names.

"I hear that you were a financial advisor in New York."

He turned to the blond woman named Kaley something. She was attractive in a too-made-up sort of way. Her jeans were a little too tight as was her tank top that carried one of those sayings that he didn't dare attempt to read.

Luckily the mayor was walking their way. He reached for her arm and pulled her into the circle. "Hello, Morgan."

"Holt, it's nice that you could make it," she told him with a smile that reminded him of Leah.

"Your sister thought it was time I met a few people."

"I, for one, am glad he came," Kaley said as she moved in a little closer.

"So am I," Morgan said. "Holt, if you have a

minute, I need to speak with you." She glanced at Kaley. "If you'll excuse us for a moment…"

Kaley frowned, but finally managed a tight smile. "I guess I can let Holt go…for a while. Maybe later we can share some refreshments."

"Maybe," Holt said as he took Morgan's arm. "What do I owe you?" he said when they found a deserted area.

"Sorry, Kaley is a little…overeager."

"You're too nice. If you hadn't shown up she'd be naming our children."

Morgan laughed. "Well, she's used to men giving her attention. But I only want to discuss a little business." She took a breath. "First, I want to say that, speaking for the town, we're glad you've decided to stay in Destiny."

"Thank you. I'm glad I'm staying, too."

"And secondly, I want to talk to you about a section of your property. Maybe Leah has already mentioned it to you."

He shook his head. "No, she hasn't said anything. So what's this about my land?"

"I'm been looking for a way to bring revenue into town, and it seems logical that we build a ski resort. The town owns an ideal parcel of land, but we just need access from the highway before we can develop the area."

"Where is this land?"

"It's Silver Wolf Pass."

Holt knew the location. It would cut right by Hidden Falls. "You want to build a road through my property?"

Morgan raised an eyebrow. "It's not as drastic as it sounds. Maybe you should come by my office so you can see the plans."

Holt didn't like being blindsided like this. Was Leah supposed to butter him up so he'd be more agreeable when approached? "Did you ever talk about this with my...with John?"

"I did, in fact."

"And what did he say to your idea?"

"I'm afraid we didn't have much time to discuss it, but he did promise to think about it."

"Well, I'm not going to think about it, because I don't want anyone building a highway across my land. Now if you'll excuse me, I need to find Corey." Holt knew he was being rude, but at this point he wasn't sure he could contain his anger. Had Leah planned to get him to agree to this?

Before he could reach her, Leah was cornered by another group of people just as the meeting was called to order.

He forced himself to take a seat, but he wasn't finished with this. He would just have to wait until he got Leah back to the ranch, then he'd set her straight.

Set everyone straight.

CHAPTER SEVEN

LATER that evening, Leah was in the ranch's kitchen when Holt finally came in from checking on Lulu. Her foal was due anytime and he'd been watching her closely.

"How's the mother-to-be doing?"

He walked to the coffeepot and poured a cup. "She's getting close. Zach's going to call when it's time."

Leah was excited. "Could I go down, too? It's been a long time since I've watched a birth."

He shrugged. "I don't have a problem with that."

He sure knew how to make a girl feel welcome. "I promised Corey he could go, too, I should wake him." He started to leave the kitchen when Leah stopped him.

"Holt, is there something wrong?"

He looked at her with that unreadable hooded gaze of his. "Why should there be something wrong?"

"Maybe because you haven't said more than a

few words to me since last night when you came into my room. I thought that…"

"You thought what?"

"I thought we could now at least talk to each other if something was bothering one of us."

He frowned and crossed the room to her. "Okay, maybe we should talk. When were you planning on telling me about the town wanting me to sell land for an access road?"

She swallowed hard. "I'd forgotten all about it."

"Were you elected to sweet-talk me into agreeing to give the town access?"

Leah was starting to get angry over his constant mistrust. "Well, whatever the plan, it seems that I've failed miserably."

"I don't like being used."

"And I don't like you thinking I would use a friend like that. Besides, all Morgan wanted me to do was present the idea to you. You have the choice to look over the plans and tell them yes or no." She threw up her hands in defeat. "Word was people in town thought you came here to sell the ranch, then head back to New York."

"Well, I'm staying," he said.

"Then prove it. Stop closing yourself away from everyone and get to know your neighbors."

He opened his mouth to protest and she stopped him. "And don't say they're just curious because you're John's son, or I'll clobber you. You are John

Rawlins's son. If you're not proud of that, there's something wrong."

Raw emotion flashed across his face. "I am tired of being compared to the man. He wasn't in my life. This ranch, this land, is all I ever had of him."

"I'm sorry about that, Holt." She stepped closer and placed her hand on his arm. "I know you never had the chance to know John, and I wish so much you had." She felt him start to pull away and she tightened her grip. "No, please listen to me. The man I knew would have loved his child—his son. There had to be something that happened between your parents to keep him away."

"Well, whatever it was, it worked. I never saw him after I left here." Holt broke free and walked out the door. As much as Leah wanted to stop him, Holt Rawlins wasn't going to listen to anything she had to say.

"Wow, look, Holt." Corey gasped. "She's getting up."

"I see," Holt said as he leaned back on the railing in the birthing pen. He was exhausted, but even more amazed at the Silver R's newest equine resident.

"That's what a foal is supposed to do," Zach said. "They got to stand up to see if everything works, that she'll be able to reach her mama to eat."

Holt watched the still-wobbly golden-chestnut filly check out her new surroundings. He wiped his hand on a towel and glanced across the gate at Leah.

"Congratulations, Dad," she told him.

Almost against his will, he found himself smiling. "Thanks. Am I supposed to hand out cigars?" He couldn't believe how a new foal could bring him such joy. Maybe it wasn't the recent birth as much as the shared experience with Corey. And Leah.

"I guess someone needs to come up with a name," Zach said. "You have any ideas, Corey?"

"You want me to name her?"

Zach exchanged a glance with Holt. "Sure."

"Her coat is all golden," Corey said.

"How about we call her *Golden Girl*?" Zach suggested.

"Goldie, for short," Corey said.

"I like that." Holt nodded. "Goldie it is."

When Corey yawned, Zach suggested they all turn in. He'd keep an eye on the filly.

Once Corey was settled in bed, Holt followed Leah into the hall, but he stopped her before she retired to her room. When she looked at him with those big eyes, he nearly forgot what he wanted to say. But he couldn't lose his nerve now.

"Leah, about earlier… I guess I jumped to conclusions before I knew the whole story."

She didn't say anything.

"You were right, I'll go and talk to your sister in a few days."

She sighed. "That's all Morgan wanted you to do in the first place. You've got to start trusting people." Leah started to turn away, but Holt stopped her.

"I wish I could change that."

Leah wanted to believe him. She wanted a lot of things. She wanted to know the man behind the armor. The same man who held her one night when she was afraid to be alone. "There's nothing wrong with admitting we need someone." Unable to stop herself, she leaned into him and rested her head against his chest. She loved the sound of his pounding heart. "Just so you know. I'm here if you need a friend."

Holt pulled back and his intense gaze locked on her. The heat between them quickly became electrifying. "Friends? Friendship is not exactly what I'm feeling for you right now."

His head lowered and his mouth covered hers. The kiss started out slow and tantalizing, then began to feed on their hunger for one another. He wrapped his arms around her waist and drew her closer, pressing his body against hers as his mouth magically caressed hers. With a moan, she parted her lips, allowing him inside.

Suddenly Holt broke off the kiss, leaving her dazed and confused. His eyes narrowed as he fought to slow his breathing. "Oh, Leah. I think we both want more than just friendship. A lot more."

The following weekend was the Silver R roundup.

It wasn't a large herd, but Holt needed help to bring the cattle in for branding. More men than

Holt had expected showed up at dawn. All Zach had told him was that he had contacted enough neighbors to get the job done. The foreman had said nothing about the men bringing their families.

By midmorning, the mamas and bawling calves had been separated into the holding pens. Up at the house another crowd had gathered, then Leah and Claire Keenan ushered the bevy of women into the house.

"Relax," Zach told Holt. "This is how we do things in Colorado. Neighbors help out neighbors."

"There are so many people. How are we going to feed all these…neighbors?"

Zach nodded toward the women, and Holt saw the answer in the parade of dishes being carried into the house. "I don't think you have to worry on that score, either. Leah and Claire have things in hand. Now, let me show you how to brand a calf."

After the next few hours Holt decided he had never been so dirty, or so tired. Since he wasn't an experienced roper, he ended up being the one who held down the calves to brand. It seemed like an easy job, but that changed after he'd gotten kicked in nearly every part of his body. Dust filled his eyes and nose, and the stench of burning fur and flesh hung in the air.

"Hey, Holt," a neighbor, Bart Young, announced. "The ladies are calling us to eat."

Holt turned to find that a number of tables had

been set up under the trees on one side of the house. One table was covered with food and some men were already in line to eat.

His stomach growled. "Then I guess we better go eat."

As the men washed under the water spigot next to the house, Holt looked around for Leah and found her with Corey. The boy had been a little help earlier, but now he was off to play with his friend, Mason.

Leah glanced over her shoulder and smiled at Holt. Sudden warmth spread through his veins clear down to his toes. The memory of their kiss the other night flashed into his mind. How he wanted to replay it again…and again. He quickly shook away the thoughts that would only get him in trouble.

"Well, look at you, Mr. Big City Boy," Leah greeted him.

"I guess I am pretty dirty."

"Ranching is a dirty business." She gave him a slow once-over. "It seems to suit you, though. How are you handling it?"

He shrugged. "Not bad, but I'll probably be black and blue by tomorrow."

"One good thing, you'll be so sore that you probably won't even notice the bruises."

They both laughed.

"You should get some food," she said.

He glanced at the heaping platters of fried

chicken, and the overflowing bowls of salads. "Zach says I have you to thank for organizing this." He took off his hat and ran a hand through his hair. "I guess I never thought about food for today."

"I figured," she said. "And since there isn't any pizza delivery out here, I called Mom and she got the women together to arrange this."

"I'm indebted to her, too."

Leah frowned. Would she ever get through to this man? "These people don't want you to feel indebted. They're doing this because John was a friend and neighbor. And I have no doubt that you'll be just as willing to help them, too. Now, you better eat. You still have work to do this afternoon."

"Only if you join me."

She hesitated. The whole town was watching their every move anyway, so why not? "Sure. I'll fix you a plate while you clean up."

"Great. Just make sure you get me some of whatever your mother made." Grinning, he started walking as he popped the snaps on his shirt.

She managed a quick glance as his broad chest came into view. Then all too soon, Holt turned away and she started for the buffet to discover the other wives smiling at her.

She ignored them. What was the big deal? So Holt had kissed her a few times. Okay, so they'd been mind-blowing kisses. There wasn't any law against that.

Leah picked up a plate, scooped up her mother's potato salad, a few deviled eggs, two pieces of chicken and a roll. She then went to find two empty chairs at the table. Going back, she got her own food, but when she returned she found another visitor had arrived at the ranch.

Kaley Sims was dressed in a hot-pink tank top and jeans. She had taken Leah's seat, but as close as she was to Holt, she might as well have been sitting in his lap.

Looking guilty, Holt stood when Leah arrived at the table. "Leah, you're back." He pulled out the chair on his other side. "Look who's here," he said as he nodded at Kaley.

"Hi, Leah," Kaley said, but her attention was on Holt.

"Kaley, what a surprise." Leah forced a smile. "Since when do you come to roundups?" She doubted the woman ever wore her boots for anything besides dancing.

With an innocent smile, Kaley leaned in closer to Holt, nearly spilling out of her tank top. "I heard that Holt was having his first roundup, and I had to bring by a pie."

"That was thoughtful of you," Holt said as he tried to concentrate on his food. "This chicken is good, Leah."

"I made it," she admitted, pretty sure that Kaley had purchased her pie at the bakery.

Kaley sighed. "Oh, Leah, you and your sisters are all such good cooks. The kitchen just isn't the room I'm the best in."

Leah choked on her food.

"Are you okay?" Holt asked.

She nodded. "Some food just went down the wrong way." She turned to the woman. "Well, if you want to help, you could stay and wash dishes."

Kaley glared at her. "I'm sorry to say I can't. I need to pick up my daughter." She stood and placed her hand on Holt's shoulder and bent her head toward him. "Maybe another time. Holt, I'm in town and in the book."

Leah clenched her fists under the table.

"Thanks for stopping by," Holt called as she walked away.

Never looking at Leah, he returned to eating. "All that work this morning makes a person hungry," he said.

Too bad Leah had lost her appetite. "It's a shame Kaley couldn't stay." She stabbed at her food. "She's so…attentive."

Holt stopped eating, a faint trace of a grin starting. "I didn't notice."

She stood. "You would have to be dead not to notice Kaley Sims."

Holt stopped her. "Will you sit down? I'm not interested in Kaley."

"I couldn't care less either way," she fibbed. "But

fair warning, Kaley always gets what she goes after…and she's coming after you."

Leah turned and marched off toward the house, hating that she'd let herself care. But she did care, darn it. Especially when she knew that Holt had a life here, and she wasn't going to be staying.

Not even her feelings for the man could change what she had to do.

By late afternoon, the last of the calves were branded and back in the pen. The men walked toward the house for a cold drink and to relax. Thanks to Leah and the other women, they had leftovers waiting along with iced tubs of soft drinks and beer.

The party began.

It wasn't by any means a wild party, everyone just sat around enjoying the quiet evening with friends and family. Holt looked for Leah and Corey and found the kid playing with his new friends. Leah talking with a group of the women.

He couldn't help but watch her. She had such an easy way with people. Everyone liked her, himself included. His gut tightened with need. Not just the physical need she'd awakened in him, but a different need he'd never experienced before. The need to see her smile…to hear her laughter…or just for the scent of her hair when she walked past him.

"Leah's grown into a pretty woman," Bart said as he appeared next to him.

"Since I didn't know her as a kid, I couldn't say. But yes, Leah is pretty."

The fiftysomething rancher handed him a longneck bottle of beer. "She was cute as a button."

The last thing Holt wanted to do was talk about his relationship with Leah. "Bart, I want to thank you for all your help today," he said, changing the subject.

"Glad to do it." The man pushed back his hat. "I guess we were all a little curious to see how you would handle your first roundup." His grin caused tiny lines to crinkle around his eyes. "Guess we can't call you a big city boy anymore. I'd be proud if you'd come and help me out at the end of the month."

His neighbor's acceptance meant a lot to Holt. "I'd be happy to," he told him. "Just tell me the time and place."

"Will do. Can you sweet talk Leah into bringing some of her fried chicken?"

Holt laughed. In the past few weeks Leah had become such a part of his life. He found he was eager to return to the house each night, knowing she would be there.

"I'll see what I can do," he told his neighbor.

Bart just winked and together they strolled back to the group that gravitated around the open pit. With the cool of the evening ahead, Zach had started a fire.

It was an opportunity to talk to everyone. "I want to thank you all for coming here today. I couldn't have done this without your help. I hope I can return the favor." He raised his bottle and smiled. "And to the lovely ladies who prepared all the delicious food. Thank you. I haven't eaten this well in years." He patted his flat stomach. "And it's a good thing."

That brought a laugh from his neighbors, and he searched the group for Leah. She was standing in the back. He found he wanted her with him.

"Does this mean that you're going to hang around?" The question came from one of the ladies.

"I think so," he said honestly. "I know I have a lot to learn, but I'm beginning to feel like I belong."

"You're John Rawlins's son. Of course you belong here."

Holt's smile froze, but he willed himself to relax. He wasn't going to let his father spoil another evening. Suddenly everyone's attention went to one of the men who pulled out a harmonica, and began to play. More leftovers were eaten and the kids roasted marshmallows.

Holt glanced at Leah, realizing with her here, this was about as perfect as it could get.

Leah went into the barn to escape. She felt like there was a spotlight on her whenever Holt looked at her. Her mother was even singing the man's praises. Leah didn't need anyone telling her what kind of man Holt Rawlins was. She already knew, and she already had feelings for him.

She walked down the center aisle to Lulu and Goldie's stall. The mare greeted her with a neigh and came to the gate.

"Hello, girl." Leah stroked Lulu's muzzle "How's it going?" She glanced down at the filly at her side. "Hi, Goldie." but the two-week-old foal skittered away when she reached out her hand. "A little shy after all the visitors today, huh?" Corey had been showing off the new addition to the ranch.

Although the filly didn't want attention, Lulu did. Leah felt comforted by petting the mare. It relaxed her, too. Today had been busy, but she loved all the work. She'd gotten to visit with people who'd been such a big part of her life.

Her life. Leah sighed. At one time, she thought she'd had it all planned out. From an early age, she'd known what she'd wanted. A career and travel first. Not until she was thirty would she even think about settling down. Now suddenly she was playing house with one sexy cowboy, and a surrogate mother to an eight-year-old boy. And she was crazy about both of them.

"So, this is where you've been hiding out," Holt said.

Leah jerked around to find him leaning against an empty stall across the aisle. Even dressed in dirty jeans and shirt from the day's branding, he looked handsome...sexy...mouthwatering.

She finally found her voice. "I was just checking on the filly."

"I think Goldie's been checked on by nearly half the town today." His smile was slow and easy and it took her breath away.

He pushed away from the stall and walked to her. "I had a feeling that you are avoiding me."

She continued to stroke the horse, but Lulu changed allegiance and went to Holt. Fickle female. The mare nudged against his hands, begging for attention and Holt began stroking her nose.

"She just can't get enough attention," he said.

Leah met his heated gaze, then recalled an earlier event that day. Several women had been immune to his charms, especially one shapely blonde. "Reminds me of someone else."

"If you're talking about Kaley, I'm not interested. She's definitely not my type."

"Who says I care?" she told him, trying to sound convincing.

Holt clutched his hand to his heart. "Oh, that hurts."

Leah worked hard not to smile. "Go cry on Kaley's shoulder." She turned serious. "Encouraged or not, the woman goes after what she wants. And she wants you."

Holt took a step closer and reached for Leah. "I don't want her."

Leah suddenly felt hot. "It's none of my business."

He leaned toward her. "Yes, it is." He brushed back a loose strand of her hair. His grazing touch caused her to shiver. "Because, Leah, you're the one who keeps me awake at night, the one who makes me ache until I think I can stand it any longer." His head descended to hers.

"Holt…this isn't a good idea…you kissing me…" Her resistance was weak; even she didn't believe her words.

Holt searched her face, the blatant desire in his green eyes caused her heart to pound in her ears. His warm breath caressed her face, making her shiver. "That's why you're going to kiss me," he whispered. "So you'll have no regrets."

Leah swallowed hard. "I still don't think this is wise…to start anything." Even she didn't believe what she was saying.

Holt touched her cheek with the back of his hand. "Don't think, Leah." His low, husky tone was slowly mesmerizing her. "Just feel…" he breathed and she lost the battle. With a tiny whimper she surrendered, went into his arms and her lips touched his.

This one time wouldn't hurt.

Now if only she believed that.

CHAPTER EIGHT

THE next day, standing on the inn's porch, preparing to snap a picture, Leah was still reliving Holt's kisses. She didn't want to think about them at all. But as hard as she tried she couldn't stop the feelings.

None of that mattered. She was heading off in a few weeks for her next assignment. That meant leaving her family and friends behind. And worse, this time it would mean leaving Holt and Corey. Although she was crazy to feel that way. She'd be a fool to expect a commitment from Holt, and Corey would probably go into a foster home soon, and there was nothing she would do about it. She sighed, feeling her eyes burn. Too bad because he and Holt were great together and needed each other badly.

"Leah, are you going to take the picture today?" Morgan called.

Leah shook away her thoughts, realizing her sister and parents were on the inn's porch waiting for her.

"Sorry, I was checking for the best light," she fibbed. "Okay, now smile." Her parents obliged and she took the picture. "That's it."

Morgan came down the steps. "Where else do you want to go?"

Leah smiled at her sister's excitement and she was glad she'd volunteered to take pictures for the town's new brochure and Web site. "How about if we call it a day? I'm losing the light and I need to get Corey back to the ranch for dinner."

Just then Corey and his new best friend, Mason, came running from the backyard. They were both wet and dirty, proof they'd been playing in the creek.

"Looks like you both have been busy," Leah said, not caring that the boy was a mess. He was smiling.

"We caught some crawdads, but put them back," Corey said.

"I, for one, am glad to hear that. We should get back to the ranch."

Just then Mason's mother, Judy Langston, pulled up. She waved and Leah went to the car. "Sorry about the condition of your son."

Judy laughed. "Don't worry, I'm used to it." She waved to her boy. "Come on, Mason. It's time to go."

"Ah, Mom, I want to play with Corey. Can he come to our house?"

Judy looked at Leah. "We'd love to have Corey spend the night." The boys began to cheer.

When Leah was unable to reach Holt by phone, she gave permission for the sleepover. After cleaning up the excited Corey, she sent him off to the Langstons's house. Then she gathered her camera and headed back to the ranch, trying not to think that she would be staying with Holt Rawlins. Alone.

By the time she reached the ranch, a tired-looking Holt was walking up from the barn.

"Where's Corey?"

"He's sleeping over at Mason's tonight," she began, then hurried on to say. "I tried to call you, but you must have been out. Mom knows the family, and Mason's mother, Judy, is very nice. She said she'd drive Corey home in the morning."

He raised a hand. "It's okay, Leah. I don't mind that you let him go." His mouth gave away a hint of a smile. "That means we get the night off. What do you say we make the most of it, and go out?"

Leah felt her heart race. A date? In public? Would that be wise? "Thank you, but I have a lot of work to do. I want to go over the pictures I took today."

"I could help you after we get back." He walked up to her. "So why don't you go and get ready?"

She knew it was a bad idea to spend any more time alone with this man, but all her logic seemed to disappear. She wanted to spend the evening with him. "What should I wear?"

"Whatever you decide will be fine." His smile widened. "But you better hurry…you've got thirty minutes."

Leah used all of the time allotted her to get ready for her date with Holt.

She managed to shower and change into an Indian-print broomstick skirt and cotton turquoise blouse, and to slip on a pair of low-heeled sandals.

With one last glance in the mirror, she checked her makeup and hair. Unable to do anything with her wayward curls, she used clips to pull the long strands away from her face. Then she drew another long breath, released it and walked to the door.

This was crazy. Why was she so nervous? She was only going out for dinner. One would think that she'd never had a date before. This was different. They'd already had an intense relationship, just living in the same house. Not to mention the fact she couldn't resist the man's kisses.

Well, starting tonight she was just going to try harder. With renewed determination, she made her way down the steps to the landing and stopped when she saw Holt in the entry. Her pulse shot up.

In a pair of dark trousers and a wine-colored shirt, he looked nothing like the rancher she'd been living with the past weeks.

He looked up at her, gave her an appreciative once-over and smiled. She felt her knees go weak.

This was bad. She managed the stairs as he came to meet her at the bottom.

He took her hand. "You are well worth the wait. You look beautiful."

She felt herself blush. "Thank you. You're not so bad yourself. You seem to have lost the rancher look."

"Do you mind?"

She inhaled his woodsy scent and felt light-headed. "No, not at all."

His smile widened. "Good." He checked his watch. "We should get going. I made reservations at Francisco's Cantina in Durango."

"Oh, I haven't been there in years," she told him as he tucked her hand under his arm and walked her out the front door.

"So I made a good choice?" he asked as he opened the door to his truck.

"A very good choice," she told him.

He leaned forward. "Good. I want tonight to be…memorable."

Holt sat across from Leah at the corner table. It was a weekday and the restaurant wasn't busy. That made him happy since he wanted some quiet time with Leah.

"Do you miss being a financial advisor?" she asked.

"Surprisingly, no. Of course, I was able to keep a few of my clients."

"Is that because you aren't sure that ranching will work out?" There was a hint of a smile.

"I have to admit when I discovered John left me the ranch, I wasn't sure what I would do." He leaned forward at the table, mesmerized by Leah framed in the soft candlelight. "I was curious more than anything."

She smiled. "I'd say you seemed to have taken over the position as rancher as if you were born to it. You handled the roundup like a pro."

"Thank you." Her praise meant a lot to him. "You should have seen me a few months ago. The three times a week in the gym didn't compare to tossing bails of hay. Zach was a big help. Never once has he given up on me, but he never let up on me, either." He smiled, realizing how much he was enjoying being with Leah. "Enough about me. Tell me about you, and your job. Have you always wanted to travel the world?"

She grew serious as she shook her head. "I've always wanted to be a photographer. And after college, I more or less fell into the job at *Our World* magazine." She frowned and took a sip of her wine. "It's hard to pass up the opportunity."

"You've made a name for yourself, you could go and work anywhere…even for yourself," he said, wishing she wasn't going to be leaving so soon.

"Maybe I will…someday."

He nodded. "You can't blame me for wanting you to stay around."

"Maybe you'll be the one who doesn't stay around. For someone who's lived in New York for so long, I'd think you'd missed the nightlife...the people.

"Sometimes," he admitted. "I enjoyed being able to go to fine restaurants and seeing a Broadway show. As for the people, I was involved in a relationship, but before I left we ended it." His gaze feasted on her. "I'm beginning to discover that Colorado has what I really want."

She smiled as her slender fingers toyed with the stem of her wineglass. "As I said before, you definitely fit in at the ranch."

Unable to resist any longer from touching her, he reached out and placed his hand over hers. "If things had been different, maybe I would have," he said. Not wanting to ruin tonight's mood, he pushed aside the old bitterness and leaned closer. "No doubt you and I would have met a lot sooner."

Leah wrinkled her nose. "And you would have run the other way. I was all braces, skinny and a tomboy."

"Oh, I would have noticed you." He threaded his fingers though hers. It felt good, and so right.

"I would have noticed you, too," she whispered.

His breath caught in his chest. "I think it's safe to say that we've definitely noticed each other now. Isn't that what counts?"

She nodded. "Too bad there isn't much time..."

He touched a finger to her lips, stopping her words. "Let's not think about what's going to happen later on. Right now is all that matters."

Nearly two hours later, Leah's heart was pounding hard as Holt parked the truck at the back door. It was only eleven, but their time together was almost over. Sadly, she realized that her time with everyone she cared about was about to come to an end, and soon.

Silently Holt climbed out, walked around the truck and opened the door. He took her hand to help her down. All at once, she lost her footing on the running board, and began to fall. She gasped as he caught her body against his and helped her to solid ground, but then he didn't release her. He held her close, so close she could feel his rapid heartbeat. Her own pulse was racing. She knew she should step away, but when his hands moved up and cradled the back of her head, she shivered.

Slowly she looked up. "We should go inside," she whispered, feeling his breath against her cheek.

"It is getting late," he agreed, his gaze never leaving hers, weakening her resolve to keep her distance—to not get involved with this man.

Leah finally lost the battle. Her hands slid up his chest and circled his neck. "Very late." It was already too late for her... She was falling in love with Holt Rawlins.

"Then maybe I should say a proper good-night."

His head lowered and his mouth covered hers in a searing kiss. She trembled at the sudden rush of desire, but quickly became a willing participant. She combed her fingers in his hair and clung to him. With a groan, he parted her lips and delved inside to taste her, but it didn't seem to be enough for either of them.

No man had ever made Leah feel like this. She'd never had the time, never found a man she wanted like this.

Holt tore his mouth away. "This is crazy," he breathed, resting his forehead against hers. "You make me crazy," he confessed, before he cupped her face and returned for another kiss.

Leah was out of her mind, too. She shouldn't allow this to happen, but she couldn't seem to stop herself.

He finally broke away. "I better get you inside."

Leah wasn't able to speak as Holt led her into the house and up the stairs. Once in front of her bedroom, he stopped and pinned her against the door for another kiss.

"If I don't stop, I won't be able to leave you." His mouth found hers again and again, finally he eased back and looked down at her. She saw her desire and need mirrored in his eyes.

Leah's grip tightened. "Don't leave me, Holt. Please."

His intense gaze searched hers. "Are you sure, Leah?"

She wasn't sure of anything but her need for

this man. She couldn't let him walk away. "Yes," she breathed and opened her bedroom door. Together they went inside and walked to the bed, illuminated by soft moonlight. Not a word was spoken as Holt began to remove her clothes, layer by layer. None was needed as his hands and lips caressed her.

Leah was in love with Holt and she wanted to show him...if only for tonight.

Dawn came too soon, Holt thought as he rolled over and looked at Leah. Her beautiful face was relaxed in sleep. They'd been up most of the night, sharing an incredible experience. Fresh feelings stirred in his gut and the sudden need for her hit him like a bolt of lightning. He hadn't seen it coming, but it got him just the same.

Just like Leah had gotten to him.

Holt suddenly smiled. Resisting the urge to kiss her awake and begin their lovemaking all over again, he slipped out of bed. Gathering up his clothes, he headed to his bedroom to shower. There was still a ranch to run and Corey would be home soon. Holt found himself grinning again. He was looking forward to the routine.

Leah released the air from her lungs, and opened her eyes the second the door clicked shut. Holt was finally gone. She didn't want to face him just yet, nor did she want to analyze her feelings. She hadn't the right to give herself to a man, knowing there couldn't be any future for them as a couple.

"But you love him," she whispered in the silent room. She closed her eyes and began reliving last night. His touch, his caresses…his mind-blowing kisses. He pleased her in every way.

That didn't change the fact that she had to leave him.

An hour later, Leah finally came downstairs to find Holt in the kitchen fixing breakfast. He glanced over his shoulder and saw her. With a smile, he crossed the room and kissed her.

"Good morning," he said.

"Good morning," she returned, and stepped out of his arms. "You shouldn't have let me sleep in."

"There wasn't any reason for you to get up. I did the chores. I would have come up to your room if you hadn't come downstairs soon." He pulled her back into his arms, and kissed her.

Leah couldn't resist him, but as much as she wanted to give this relationship a chance, she knew she couldn't. She finally moved away. "Holt, about last night…"

"It was incredible," he finished for her.

"Yes, it was." She was dying inside. "But we have to think about Corey."

Holt could see Leah's uneasiness, and he didn't

like it. "So we need to set a good example for the kid, huh?"

She nodded. "We jumped in pretty fast and… what happened last night can't happen again. I'm leaving soon…"

Her words were interrupted when the phone rang.

Holt wanted to ignore the call, but it could be about Corey. He went to answer it. "Hello,"

"Hello, this is Joy Bryant, the editor for *Our World* magazine. I'm looking for Leah Keenan. Her mother gave me this number."

Holt's gut tightened. He wanted to say he'd never heard of Leah Keenan, but knew that wouldn't stop what was about to happen.

"One moment." He held out the receiver. "It's your editor."

The look on Leah's face showed her surprise. "I need to take this," she said, and carried the cordless phone out of the kitchen and into the office.

Holt went to the stove and turned off the flame. Breakfast was the last thing he wanted, not when his life was suddenly on hold.

Within minutes, Leah came back in and hung up the phone. "My editor wants me to go next week. There's been an uprising."

He waved off her words. "Isn't there always an uprising? Somewhere? Surely you told them you can't go now."

She shook her head. "This is my job, Holt. How could I tell her that? Besides it's only for a few weeks."

"What are you going to do? Drop in between assignments?" He glared at her. "Don't you deserve some time off to be with your family—to be with Corey." He left out himself as the familiar feelings of rejection nearly overwhelmed him. How could he have been foolish enough to let himself care again? "I guess he doesn't matter."

She blinked, not able to hide the hurt. "How can you say that? Of course I care, but you knew I was going back. How important this is to me."

"There are other people who need you, Leah. What about Corey?" Holt refused to let her know how much he'd gotten accustomed to having her here every day. Needing her to be here. For him.

"Corey has you and Zach."

"So that's your excuse for copping out on us."

"I have a few days before I need to leave. By then Corey will be used to the idea."

Holt doubted it. "Maybe you shouldn't stay here until then. Just cut the cord now."

Holt watched her as she swallowed hard. "If that's what you want. I can be packed and gone in an hour." She blinked. "If you don't mind, I'd like to see Corey and tell him about my new assignment."

"You can pick him up from his sleepover."

Leah nodded and turned to leave, but paused. "I know you won't believe this, Holt, but I'll never

forget you. Both you and Corey mean a lot to me."
With that she hurried out of the room.

"Just not enough," he whispered to the empty
room. Even busying himself with fixing breakfast,
he could still hear her moving around upstairs.

A few minutes later, he heard her come downstairs, then the front door closed. He had to stop
himself from going after her. What good would it
do? She'd still leave. Carrying his food to the table,
he sat down. A car door slammed and the engine
started. Then there was only the sound of her
driving away.

It was over. Leah was gone. Now, if he could just
get rid of her memory. He closed his eyes and immediately saw her smile…heard her laughter. She'd
touched every corner in this house…and in his
heart.

Now it was all empty.

"But I don't want you to leave," Corey said, tears
in his voice.

Leah turned away from the highway and looked
at the boy in passenger seat. "It's my job, Corey. I
have to go. I'll get back as soon as I can." His sad
face broke her heart. "You'll have Holt and Zach
here for you." She prayed she wasn't lying. "They
aren't leaving you. And we can e-mail and write
letters to each other."

The boy looked panicked and she couldn't blame

him. His life was about to be turned upside down…once again. How could he believe anyone?

"Are you really coming back?"

She hoped this assignment was only three weeks as her editor promised, but she knew there were no guarantees. "Really. I told my editor that I can't miss my parents' anniversary party." Steering the car off the highway and into ranch property. Time was running out and she needed to tell Corey the rest of it. "And since I'm leaving so soon, I've moved back with my parents at the inn."

She saw the panic on his face. "But why can't you stay here with us?"

Because she couldn't deal with Holt—seeing his caring turn to hatred. She wished things could be so different. If he loved her…if she hadn't made a promise she couldn't break. "It's just that I haven't spent much time with my parents and sister. I'll be seeing you, too."

"You promise?"

She parked at the back door, and turned in her seat. "I promise, Corey." She reached for him and pulled him into a big hug. She couldn't believe how much this little boy had come to mean to her. "I won't forget you."

He pulled back. "I won't forget you, either," he said. "I just wish you and Holt could stay with me…forever and ever," he cried. Embarrassed, he swiped the tears off his cheeks and slowly climbed out of the car.

She watched him take off toward the barn where Holt appeared in the doorway. He greeted the child with a quick hug, but never took his gaze off her. For a spilt second, Leah wanted to be the one running to him. Instead she backed up the car and drove away before she changed her mind.

The next day, Holt's mood only worsened. Corey spent the evening asking him questions he couldn't answer. He almost drove into town to face Leah himself, but what good would it do? She'd made her decision, and he wasn't a part of her future.

Zach walked in the back door. "What's for lunch?"

"Whatever you intend to fix. I'm not hungry."

The foreman went to the sink and started washing his hands. "I see you're still grumpy as an old grizzly."

"Sorry. Just for you, I'll try to sweeten my mood."

Zach grabbed the towel and dried his hands. "Look, none of us are happy about Leah leavin'. She means a lot to all of us, but at least we should make an effort for the boy. He wants to spend the afternoon with Mason. Since you've been in such a great mood, I told him he could go."

Holt nodded. "That's probably a good idea."

"Maybe a little time to yourself will help you get

your priorities straight. I could be wrong, but I thought you had feelings for Leah." The old man arched an eyebrow, waiting for an answer.

Holt didn't have one, nor had he a chance to analyze his feelings for Leah. He knew one thing—he couldn't put the boy in the middle of this. Holt had to put his personal feelings aside, and make his first concern Corey, and how this affected him.

Before he could respond there was a knock at the back door. Holt went to answer it and found the social worker, Lillian Gerard, standing on the porch.

"Hello, Mrs. Gerard," he said as he opened the screen door and allowed her to step inside.

"Mr. Rawlins," she greeted him. "I apologize for not calling before coming out, but I was in the area and decided to take the chance you would be here."

What did she need to visit him for? "I'm usually around or close by." He escorted her into the kitchen. "You remember my foreman, Zach Shaw."

"Hello, ma'am." Zach nodded, but stayed across the room.

"Nice to see you again, Zach."

They all stood there in an uneasy silence until Holt finally asked, "May I offer you some coffee?"

She shook her head. "No, thanks, I really don't have the time. I have another appointment to go to." She sighed. "I just wanted to tell you in person that a foster home has come available for Corey."

Holt's heart jump into his throat. They were taking Corey away from him, too. "Really. It happened pretty fast. Who is this family? Where is this home located?"

"It's a nice family in Durango. They have a boy about Corey's age. Their last foster child was recently returned to his family. I think this is a good solution, Mr. Rawlins." Her warm hazel eyes met his. "Unless…you can think of something else."

Holt wanted to demand to keep Corey with him, but deep down he knew it wasn't what was best for the boy. He couldn't give him…a family. "No. My only concern is that Corey be happy."

"I understand." There was another long pause. "How about I stop by tomorrow and we'll talk about it with him?"

Tomorrow was too soon. "Okay." After walking her to the door Holt stood there until the social worker drove away, feeling more alone than ever.

Zach just stared at him, then finally he asked. "You're just gonna let them take the boy?"

Holt tried to act unconcerned. "There isn't a choice here, Corey has to go."

"Says who?" Zach argued. "You could keep him yourself."

It had surprised Holt how many times over the past few weeks he'd thought the same thing. "That's a crazy idea. I have no idea how to be a father." All his own insecurities rushed to the surface, and he couldn't push them aside. "It isn't as if I had much of an example."

Anger flashed in the older man's face. "You know, since you've come here all you've done is bad-mouth your father."

Holt only stared at Zach.

"That's right, John Rawlins was your father. The best man I ever knew—ever could know. I truly thought when you decided to stay here and listened to stories about him, you'd feel differently. John was a good man. But he was also a sad, devastated man because he'd lost what mattered more to him than anything else. You."

Holt didn't want to hear this. "Too bad I never knew that man," he told him sarcastically.

"It goes both ways, son. Did you ever wonder why he never saw you?"

More years than he wanted to count, he said silently.

"So as an adult, why didn't you confront John— ask him why he never came to see you?"

"What was the use? He didn't want me."

Zach released a long sigh. "You know, it's about time you got to meet the man you despise so much." The foreman motioned for Holt to follow as he walked out of the kitchen, through the house and upstairs, all the way to the door that led to the attic. The old man turned on a light, and climbed another series of steps.

PATRICIA THAYER   151

Curious, Holt followed, brushing away cobwebs as he kept up with the old guy. Zach maneuvered around old furniture and arrived at a stack of boxes against the wall. Surprised, Holt saw his name printed on the side of one of them.

"Here it is," Zach said as he slid out a crate, reached inside and took out a shoe box, then handed it to Holt. "Go ahead, open it. I dare you to find out who John Rawlins really was." The old man turned and left Holt alone.

Holt realized his hands were shaking as he pulled off the lid. Inside he found dozens of letters tied in bundles. All were addressed to him at his mother's home, and all were stamped Return To Sender.

They were unopened.

CHAPTER NINE

HOLT hadn't gotten any of them.

Not one.

For a long time, he just stared at the letters. Unopened. Then he decided he had to know the truth about his father once and for all. He pulled one of the oldest postmarked letters from when he'd been five.

His hands shook as he unfolded the aged paper. The first letter was printed in big block letters.

Dear Holt,

I miss you a lot. I hope you like your first year at school. I hope you can come and visit me this summer. Zach and Buddy miss you, too.

Love, Dad

Buddy. The golden retriever puppy his father brought home to him one day. A dozen other long buried memories flashed into his head, of other happy times with John Rawlins.

Holt searched through dozens of letters, checking each date. His father had written him a letter a week. Holt went through the entire box. Never failing, John's letters went out on schedule at the end of every week...for the first few years, then they slowed to about once a month.

Holt spent the next two hours going over years of letters. Each year one that had been dated September, his father asked about his school. Every May he discussed plans for Holt to come and spend the summer with him.

"Why didn't I?" Holt whispered in the musty attic. "Why didn't I get to visit my father?"

Through box after box Holt continued his search for the truth. He found more personal things. The divorce decree, along with another legal paper. "A restraining order," he read aloud. "John Rawlins is restrained to within fifty yards of Elizabeth Rawlins, or their minor son, Holt Rawlins."

Holt struggled to relax, to breathe. Either this paper was phony or his mother had lied to him for years. There was one other possibility—his father had been abusive to his mother...and to him.

Holt had only vague memories of his father. His mother had refused to talk about him. She never wanted her ex-husband's name mentioned in front of Grandfather Pershing.

Holt thought back to his grandfather and how many times he'd spoken about his close friend, Judge Harold Clayton. Surely his grandfather wouldn't... Holt tore through the document to the back page and scanned down to the signature, Harold J. Clayton.

The pain he felt was overwhelming. He went to the one small dormer window and struggled with the aged sash. It finally opened, and he gulped in much needed air.

Until his grandfather's death a few years ago, everything had always revolved around Mackenzie Pershing and his wishes. His only daughter had never crossed him, except maybe once...when she married John Rawlins.

How hard had Elizabeth Pershing Rawlins tried to make up to her father for that mistake?

Holt took another gulp of air as Zach climbed the steps and poked his head into the attic. "You okay, son?" he asked.

"Why didn't you tell me about these before?"

"John asked me not to."

Holt could barely control the rush of emotions. "But all those years...all that time I could have known him, spent time with him." Tears blurred his vision and he turned away.

Zach went to him. "John did come to see you. Many times. He parked across the street from your grandparents' house and waited for a glimpse of you. He'd come back here and talk about you for days. How much you'd grown…how much you looked like your namesake, Grandfather Holt."

"But what about after I was an adult? Why didn't he come to me? Tell me he wanted to get to know me…"

The foreman sighed. "He was there the day you graduated from that fancy school, but he ran into your mother. She was furious, and told him it was too late to try to start up a father/son relationship. That you hated him."

Was it true? For years, he had hated his father. But he never knew… "All these years, I thought he didn't want me."

Zach searched Holt's face. "John had a powerful love for you. After that day at your graduation, he thought he couldn't be a part of your life…ever. He finally gave up the hope of having you back." The older man shook his head. "I was so worried about him. Then one day Leah Keenan showed up here." Zach smiled as if he were remembering. "She could never replace you as his child, but she brought sunshine into his life. Just like she's brought it into yours."

Leah had been trying to pack for her trip all morning, but her heart wasn't in it. For the past twenty-four hours all she could think about was Holt.

And their night together…

They both knew they'd shared something so special. And yet, Holt couldn't understand why she had to leave. That was why she hadn't wanted to get involved with him. Why she hadn't wanted to care…

There was a knock on the door and her mother peered inside. The look on her face showed she wasn't happy her daughter was leaving, either. "How are you coming with the packing?"

"Fine. I can only take a duffel bag and my camera bag. So I just need to make sure I have plenty of clean socks and underwear."

"Just what a mother wants to hear." Claire sat down on the edge of the bed. "I wish you didn't have to go. I feel I haven't had much time with you."

Leah felt the same. "We've talked about this, Mom. I have to go. It's my job." She stuffed two more bundled pairs of socks into the duffel's pocket.

"I would usually agree with you, if I felt your heart was in it," Claire Keenan said. Her knowing gaze locked on her daughter's. "Can you say it is, Leah?"

Leah closed her eyes. No, her heart wasn't in it. "I made a promise," she whispered. "I have to help the children."

At the knock on the door, they both turned to find her father, holding the cordless phone. "There's a call for you. It's Jason Mitchell, he's from the Mitchell Gallery in New York."

Leah frowned. She didn't have any idea who this man was. She took the phone. "This is Leah Keenan."

"Hello, Ms. Keenan, my name is Jason Mitchell. I hope I didn't call at a bad time."

"Actually this isn't really a good time, I'm just about to leave for my next assignment."

"Then I apologize for disturbing you," he said. "If I may have the name of your agent, I will contact him or her directly."

"My agent?" she asked.

"Yes. Holt neglected to give me the name when he sent me your photos."

"Holt? He sent you my photos?"

"Yes. I'm sure you've heard this before, but you have an incredible talent, Ms. Keenan. Those photos of the children were both beautiful and heart-wrenching."

Holt had sent her photos to a gallery in New York? She shook her head. "You're interested in my photos?"

"Very much so," Mr. Mitchell said. "And if you have any others I could see, I would love to look at them. The reason I called was, I do a show featuring debut artists every September. If it's possible I'd like you to participate."

This was a dream come true. "Could I get back to you on this, Mr. Mitchell?" Her mother handed her a pen and paper to jot down the gallery owner's private number before she hung up.

"The Mitchell Gallery in New York wants my photos in their next fall show," she told her parents.

"Oh, Leah, that's wonderful," her mother said and hugged her.

Next her father gave her a big bear hug. "We're so proud of you."

"Holt sent him my photos," she said, still amazed at the fact.

"Sounds like Holt is pretty proud of you, too." Tim exchanged a look with his wife. "I'll be downstairs if you need me," he said and left the two women alone.

Leah couldn't think about Holt, or how much she cared about him. "Oh, Mom, what am I going to do?" she sobbed. "I have to go back, but…"

"Sweetheart," Claire said. "You have no idea how much your pictures have helped tell the world about those children's struggles."

"But I lost Soraya."

Her mother's gaze searched hers. "It wasn't your failure. It was the cruelty of nature. You did everything you could to save her."

Leah sank back on the bed. "I wanted to give her so much."

"And you were able to…for a short time anyway. Some times these things happen for a reason." Claire took her daughter's hand. "Do you ever wonder why you were the one who found Corey…and Holt that day?"

Leah thought back to the first time she'd seen Holt. How angry and distant he'd been. And Corey…he'd been so afraid to let anyone close. "They need each other."

"They need you, too," her mother told her, tears filling her eyes also.

Leah knew her mother had to be thinking about when she took in three little girls. "Like Morgan, Paige and I needed you and Dad."

Claire nodded. "Sometimes…things happen for a reason." She squeezed her daughter's hand. "There was a reason you girls were brought to us. And there's a reason you came into Soraya's life and Corey's…and yes, Holt's."

Leah couldn't speak.

"If you'd do a show with your photos, the money you make could be used to help children."

For the first time in a long time, Leah felt hopeful.

Claire raised an eyebrow. "It's not a sin, Leah, to put your heart over your head. What do you want to do?"

Leah wanted Holt to love her. "To stay here and help Corey. But I'm afraid that isn't possible. Holt doesn't want me…"

Her mother sighed. "Holt has had a lot of rejection in his life. It's hard for him to show his feelings."

Her mother's warm gaze met hers. "But it seems to me the man has already shown his heart to you. Don't you think you should offer yours to him?"

"What if it's too late?"

"What if it isn't?" her mother challenged. "You don't have anything to lose. And there's a big chance you might gain everything you want."

Her parents had that kind of love. "I want what you and Dad have."

Claire stood. "Then it doesn't matter who is right or wrong. Holt isn't going to care who makes the first move. Only that you loved him enough to go to him."

Her mother was right. She did love Holt and she wasn't going to let him give up on them. Not without a fight.

Leah arrived at the ranch in less than twenty minutes, still afraid that she might talk herself out of it. She'd rehearsed everything she wanted to say to Holt, but by the time she went into the kitchen, she'd forgotten it all.

Expecting to see Holt, she was surprised to find Zach fixing some coffee.

"Leah, you came back," he said with a smile.

She hoped she had. To stay. "Is Holt here?"

Zach nodded. "I was just going to take him some coffee. I bet he'd rather you did it." He held out the mug to her.

She took it. "Is he in the office?"

"No, in the attic. He's going over some old letters." Kind hazel eyes held hers. "I think it's safe to say that he could use a friend right now."

Leah wasn't sure that Holt would consider her a friend right now, but she took Zach's direction and went to find him. Outside the attic door, she hesitated, released a long breath before making her way up the last section of steps. At the top, she found Holt sitting on the floor, with stacks of papers around him.

"Hey, Zach, did you know that John had boxed in the Navy?" Holt said. When he didn't get an answer, he turned around. "Leah…" He got to his feet.

Leah wanted to run, but forced herself to walk to him. "Hi."

"This really isn't a good time," he told her.

Seeing the sadness in his eyes, she wouldn't let him push her away. "Zach sent up some coffee." She handed Holt the mug and glanced around at the scattered papers on the floor. "What are you digging through?"

He shrugged. "Just some old letters."

Leah knelt down, picked one up and read the name. It was addressed to Holt. Her gaze went to the corner of the envelope. They were from John Rawlins. There were dozen more of them strewn around the floor, all were stamped, Return To Sender.

"These are from your father…" she whispered

and looked up at Holt. His jaw was rigid, his body tense, but his eyes told her of a boy's years of loneliness, a boy who had needed a father, who had wished for his father every day of his life…

"Oh, Holt." She rose and went to him, but he raised a hand to stop her from getting too close.

"Funny isn't it," he began. "All these years I've worked up a good hate for the man…" His voice quivered and he turned away momentarily. "And now, I find out that all he wanted was…his son."

Leah swallowed hard to keep her own emotions in check.

Suddenly anger slashed across his face. "I hope to God it was my grandfather sending back the letters…" He shook his head. "I don't want to think my own mother kept me from my father, but…it really doesn't matter now. Dammit! It's too late."

"It does matter, Holt," Leah insisted. "It matters that you know your father tried to stay in touch with you. That he loved you."

"And thanks to my grandfather's money and power, he managed to stop him."

She wanted to absorb his pain. "Oh, Holt, I'm so sorry—for you, for John and what you both lost. A parent should never be kept from his child." She stepped into his arms.

Like an anchor, Holt wrapped his arms around Leah. She felt so good. And she'd come back. "At least I now know the truth."

She looked up at him. "Now, you have to let go of your anger, Holt. Don't let it consume your life. That's the last thing that John would want for you."

Holt couldn't think right now, he only knew that he didn't want to lose Leah again. "It's hard for me…"

He was so torn up inside, and didn't know if he'd ever recover. "You've always said that John was a good man. I've learned that he'd come to see me every summer. He'd park across the street from my house for a chance to see me, and he even was at my graduation."

"Sounds like he loved you a lot."

His grip tightened. "If only I'd known, if only I had the chance—"

Leah placed her finger against his lips. "Holt, it wasn't your fault. It was your grandfather who kept you from your father. John knew that. And he'd be the last person who would want you to blame yourself."

"But things could have been so different." His voice was rough. "I could have known my father."

"You have these letters, Holt. Years and years of letters to learn about him. How wonderful is that?"

He worked hard to smile. "You've been his champion from the beginning."

"John was easy to love. I cared a lot about him."

"He cared for you, too." Holt leaned closer. "You're hard to resist." His gaze searched her lovely face and he reached out and touched her cheek. "And I haven't been able to," he said breathlessly.

"You haven't?"

He shook his head. "I never should have let you walk away." His head dipped and his lips touched hers. "I should have understood how much your job meant to you. I'm sorry."

"My, it seems as if you've acquired a lot of insight in the short span of twenty-four hours," she said.

"In the past few hours, I've learned more about my father and myself than I ever have before." Holt hurried to get the rest of the words out. "I've never been good at relationships, Leah. In fact I've been pretty good at running from them. I've always ended things first, so not to get hurt." He paused. "Until you, now you're going to leave, too."

Leah could barely speak, she could barely breathe as she waited for Holt to say what she longed to hear. "I wasn't leaving you, Holt, I was…"

He stopped her words when his mouth captured hers, and she forgot everything except this man and how much she cared about him.

She broke away. "Holt, I can't think when you're kissing me, and we need to talk."

"I think we need to do more of this." He kissed her cheek and made his way down her neck. "We've already wasted too much time…"

It wasn't her resistance that finally stopped him, but the footsteps on the stairs. They turned to find Zach's apologetic look. "I hate to disturb you, but I can't find Corey."

Holt stood, pulling Leah to her feet. "He went to Mason's house."

"No, he didn't. Mason's mother just phoned. Seems Corey called his friend a few hours ago and said he had a stomachache."

"Have you checked the barn? Lulu and Goldie's stall?" Holt asked.

Zach nodded. "I've searched inside and out and all the usual places."

"When was the last time you saw him?" Leah asked.

"Right before lunch," Zach said. "I was coming to the house. Corey was, too, just as soon as he finished straightening up the tack room. Remember? That was when Mrs. Gerard showed up."

Holt cursed. "Damn. He must have overheard her."

"What?" Leah asked. "Why was Lillian Gerard here?"

The two men exchanged a glance. "They found a foster home for Corey."

Leah's temper flared. "You were going to let Corey go into a foster home?"

"I didn't want to, but…you were leaving." Holt rubbed his hand over his jaw. "I thought it was the best for him. A family."

"Are you so dense that you don't know how much that boy cares for you?" She threw up her arms. "Of course, you don't, you don't even realize how much you care about him." She sighed. "Men!"

She started down the stairs, and Holt and Zach following her.

"Wait, we need to find him," Holt called.

Leah kept going until she reached the kitchen. "Yes, we do, but this time I'm calling the sheriff for help." When Holt didn't stop her, she picked up the phone. After talking to Reed Larkin, she looked at the two men. "Reed's on his way."

Holt and Zach headed for the back door. "We're going to saddle the horses," Holt said over his shoulder.

"I'm going, too," she called after him.

Holt stopped, and their gazes met. "I wouldn't leave without you, Leah. We're in this together."

Her heart suddenly started pounding. "I'm not going anywhere, either."

"You're sure?" he asked.

She couldn't trust her voice, but managed a nod.

Holt closed the distance between them and pulled her into his arms, holding her close. "We'll find him, Leah, then we need to sit down and talk…about our future."

CHAPTER TEN

HALF the town showed up at the ranch, wanting to help in the search. Neighbors came by on horseback and rode along the foothills. Some had four-wheel drive vehicles covering the ground through the pastures.

Sheriff Larkin had organized the groups of trackers. "Look, we're going to be losing daylight in about three hours, and the last thing we want is for anyone else to get lost. So keep checking in."

The word came back to the house that the abandoned mines were clear and there was no sign of the boy. There weren't any sightings of Corey. Anywhere.

Holt knew that the boy hadn't taken much in the way of food and clothes, and soon, he'd be cold when the temperature dropped. Although it was early summer, the mountains were downright chilly at night.

He had to find the boy. He had to tell Corey that he wasn't going to be abandoned ever again.

"We'll find him, Holt," Leah assured him. "The one good thing is Corey knows how to take care of himself."

"But I let him down," Holt told her, knowing he'd blamed his own father for the same thing. "He thinks I don't care. And all I wanted was for him to have a chance at a family."

"You can tell him that when we find him," Leah said, wishing that Holt had included her in the commitment.

Standing on the back porch, he raked his fingers through his hair and set his hat back on his head. "I can't just stay here, I've got to go search for him."

Leah followed Holt. She was just as frustrated, and scared. "Then I'm going with you."

After telling the sheriff of their plans, she followed Holt to their mounts, Rusty and Daisy, tied next to the barn. They'd been out earlier searching close to the house hoping to catch a break on Corey's whereabouts, but found nothing. This time they were expanding their search.

During the silent ride, Leah glanced over at Holt and saw his pain. She felt it, too. She loved Corey. She remembered the first day she'd seen the dirty eight-year-old trying to wash at the waterfall—

"Hidden Falls! Holt, I think that's where Corey went. To the falls!"

Holt glanced at her, then reached for his radio,

and relayed the message back to the sheriff. Then he turned to her. "Let's go have a look."

Ten minutes later, Holt tied the horses to a tree. He took Leah's hand and together they walked toward the falls. Holt heard the rushing sound of water, and as they passed the trees, he caught sight of the glistening water pouring over the cliff's ledge. His grip on Leah's hand tightened as they made their way across several of the large boulders and came up to the pond.

"Do you see him anywhere?" he asked Leah as they scanned the area.

"No, but he's here, Holt," Leah insisted. "I can feel it. That little stinker probably planned for us to come after him. Oh, I don't care. I just want him safe."

Holt's gaze searched her face. "You love him, too, don't you?"

"Yes," she said. "I should never have even thought about leaving him. Now, I just want another chance to tell him."

Suddenly a small figure caught his eye, and hope returned. Holt leaned down and pulled Leah close. "It seems you were right…Corey did come here."

"Really?" Leah gasped, but Holt refused to release her.

"He's hiding behind a rock just over your right shoulder."

Leah tried to slow her breathing. "What should we do?" she asked, afraid that he would run off again.

"I'm going to try not to spook him," he said as he helped her sit down on the boulder.

"You can't let him run off again."

Holt glanced over her shoulder. "I can see him, but before I call him out, I need to be able to offer him stability. A permanent home." His gaze lowered to her. "Did you mean what you said about wanting another chance with Corey?"

"Of course I did."

"What about me?" he asked. "Will you give me a second chance?"

Her eyes darkened and she swallowed hard. "Do you want another chance?"

"I want as many as it takes to convince you." He lowered his head, brushed a kiss against her mouth.

Leah wanted, and needed his words. "So you want me to stay here? Just to help you with Corey."

"That's not all I want," he said in a husky voice. "I want us as close as two people can get…I love you, Leah…"

"Oh, Holt. I love you, too." She wrapped her arms around his neck and kissed him.

With a groan, he released her. "I'd like nothing more than to show you how much I want you, but there are things we need to talk about first."

She nodded.

He stole a look toward the boulder making sure Corey was still there. "I want you to stay here, but I had no right to expect you to give up your job.

You're an incredible talent, Leah. I'll support you all the way."

"Is that why you sent my photos to Jason Mitchell?"

He was busted. "I was trying to show you other options to help the children. So Jason called you, huh?"

"This morning. He wants me to do a show in the fall."

"I knew he would love your photos." He paused a moment. "So are you thinking about it?"

"It could be a good way to raise money for a good cause."

Holt cupped her face in his hands, looking into her golden-brown eyes, hoping he'd have the privilege for the next sixty years. "You're not going overseas?"

"I haven't had a chance to talk to my boss, but I'm staying in Destiny. My very wise mother helped me understand that there is a child right here who needs me."

"Us," he corrected, not as sure of his words. "You and me, together. I need you, too, Leah."

"Together."

"Sounds good," he said, but his happiness quickly turned to worry. "Now, we just have to convince one little boy that we want him to be part of our family."

"Just talk to him, Holt. He thinks of you as his father already."

"Then I should act like one and tell him how I feel."

He kissed her nose and stood. "Corey, we know you're back there," he called out loud over the sound of the waterfall. "You might as well show your face and talk to us. We're not going away."

Holt held his breath praying he'd said the right things.

"Just go away," the boy called back. "You don't want me anymore, and I'm not going back to another foster home."

"I'm not leaving you," Holt told him. "I admit I made a mistake, thinking I was giving you what you needed. For a while I thought I couldn't be a good dad to you." His throat tightened as Leah stood beside him and took his hand, giving him courage and support. "Then I realized that I can give you a good home, myself and…love."

The seconds ticked by and finally Corey climbed on top of the boulder. "You really want to give me all that?"

"Yes, I do."

The boy straightened. "What if you get mad at me?"

"Of course I'll get angry at you, just like you'll get angry at me. That's what happens in families. I didn't have a real family myself, not until you and Leah came into my life." He stared at the boy in dirty jeans and a shirt. No doubt, he'd been in a cave. "Nothing can stop how I feel about you, Corey. I love you, son."

He watched as the boy swiped at his check, but still he didn't move off the rock. "My dad isn't going to get out of jail for a long, long time."

"Then you'll stay with me for a long, long time. I'd like it to be permanent."

"Really?" Corey asked, the sound of hope in his voice.

"I want nothing more than for you to live with me."

"What about Leah?" he asked. "Does she want a family, too?"

The kid was a born negotiator. "I want her to be part of our family, too." Holt bit back a smile as he glanced down at Leah's loving gaze.

"You better ask her," Corey said.

Holt nodded, unable to take his eyes off her lovely face. "I love you, Leah," he whispered so only the two of them could hear. He brought her hand to his lips and kissed it. "I think I have since that day I found you here. I know I can be stubborn and moody, but one thing will never change, my love for you. Will you marry me? Will you be my wife?" he asked, then quickly added. "Just so you know…Corey and I are a package deal."

Leah never knew she could ever feel this way. She leaned into Holt's solid body and pressed her palm against his fast beating heart. "I happen to think that's a good deal. Yes, I'll marry you, Holt Rawlins, and I want nothing more than to be Corey's mother."

Holt kissed her hard and fast, then grinned as he looked at Corey. "She said yes," he called.

Corey pumped his fist in the air, and cheered. That's all Holt saw because he was concentrating on his bride-to-be. He lowered his head and his mouth covered hers as he tried to relay his feelings to her.

They broke apart just as Corey made his way to them. Leah watched as Holt scooped the boy up in his arms and hugged him close.

"Don't you ever run away again." He set the boy on his feet. "You scared us."

Corey pulled back. "I'm sorry. I won't do it again."

Leah hugged him, too. "They're going to have to fight us both, because we aren't letting you go. We're a family now."

All three of them turned around just as the sheriff's four-wheel drive vehicle pulled up and Reed Larkin, Leah's parents and Lillian Gerard climbed out. A few of the neighbors rode up on horseback.

Corey stiffened. "Uh-oh, are we in trouble?"

"No, son, you're not in trouble."

The first person to greet them was Mrs. Gerard. "Hello, Corey." She looked over his soiled clothes. "Looks like you had quite an adventure."

"Hi, Mrs. G." He stood close to Holt. "I'm sorry I made everybody worry, but it's okay 'cause Holt and Leah want to be my parents."

"I'm glad that everyone is safe." The social worker turned to Holt. "Am I to take it that you've changed your mind about being foster parents?"

"Yes, Leah and I want to keep Corey with us. But we want to change his status to permanent."

"Do you agree?" The social worker smiled when Leah nodded. "I'll start on the paperwork as soon as I get back to my office."

Leah felt Holt's arm around her shoulders as he spoke to the crowd. "I want to thank everyone for helping us find our boy, and to invite everyone to our wedding."

"Yeah, we're all getting married," Corey cheered.

The groups cheered and rancher Bart Young stepped forward and shook his hand. "Congratulations, Holt. I'm glad everything worked out with the boy." The rancher paused. "John would be proud of you."

"Thanks. I'm pretty proud to be his son, too."

Leah saw the emotion flash over Holt's face. She knew more than anyone how much that meant to him. She also knew how much family meant to him.

CHAPTER ELEVEN

Two weeks later on a perfect June evening, Holt stood on the ranch porch looking at the San Juan Mountains. In another hour the engagement party would start. Leah and the other Keenan women were inside finishing the last of the details. He decided it was best to stay out of the way and came outside.

In the past fourteen days, Holt had done a lot of soul searching. Not about his feelings for Leah. They were crystal clear. He loved her more than life. He'd been getting to know himself, and he'd done that by getting to know John Rawlins. He'd read every letter from his father. Every single one that he'd never received over the last eighteen years. He'd shared them with Leah, and together they'd laughed, and cried over what he'd missed with his father.

The hardest part had been when Holt confronted his mother. At first, she'd tried to deny what happened, then in a tearful confession she'd implicated her father, saying that he'd threatened to send both her and Holt away if John Rawlins was ever involved in their lives. She'd admitted that the restraining order involved a drummed up charge and was issued by a judge who'd been a friend of his grandfather. Holt refused to allow his mother to blame Mackenzie Pershing entirely. She had the ability to change the situation, to let Holt see his father.

Elizabeth Rawlins begged her son to forgive her and return to New York. Holt refused to return. Ever. He hadn't mentioned Leah or Corey. He wasn't willing to share that information with her. Maybe someday, but not yet.

Holt had also spent the past two weeks trying to legally adopt Corey. It hadn't been easy. First, he needed permission from the boy's biological father, Roy Haynes. Holt had gone to see him in prison and assured him that this was best for his son.

Surprisingly Mr. Haynes had agreed.

Holt then hired a lawyer, and once the paperwork was completed and the waiting period was over, Corey would be Holt and Leah's son. That was amazing for someone who'd once prided himself on being a loner.

Holt studied the same mountain range that his father had looked at over his lifetime. He felt John's presence here. A peace came over Holt. This was where he belonged. This was his home.

It was still rough. He'd always regret that as a kid he hadn't known his father, but knew he wasn't alone any longer. He had Leah, and soon, they'd be married. He took a small velvet box from his pocket. They weren't officially engaged yet…not until she got a ring.

"So this is where you've been hiding."

Hearing Leah's voice, he smiled. He slipped the box back into his pocket and turned to face his future bride. "I'm not hiding. I just needed a few quiet minutes before all the guests arrive."

As usual Leah looked beautiful. Tonight she wore a pale pink dress that fitted her petite frame perfectly, allowing layers of soft lace to float from her tiny waist to midcalf. Her shiny hair was pulled up and curls framed her face.

She frowned. "It's only a party, Holt. These people are friends and neighbors and they want to celebrate with us."

"I know, but I've always hated being the center of attention."

"Oh, you foolish man." She smiled. "Don't you know? All the attention is on the bride-to-be."

"As it should be. You look spectacular."

"It must be because I'm so happy." She moved into his arms. "I love you, Holt Rawlins."

He kissed her. "I love you, too, soon-to-be Leah Rawlins."

Despite his words Leah sensed that something

was bothering Holt. Maybe he was having second thoughts. Her chest tightened at the thought.

"Holt, if this is happening too fast… I mean it's only been a little over a month since we met. We could postpone—"

Holt's mouth came down on hers, his hunger an absolute denial of her suggestion. He finally broke off the kiss, but he didn't release her. "You and Corey are the two things that have kept me sane." His green eyes held hers. "It's been your love and patience that's helped me through this rough time. I won't survive if I have to wait much longer. I dream about you, every day walking around the house, going to bed with you every night, and us waking up every morning…together."

Leah touched his face. "I'm glad you're as anxious as I am. I've been miserable living in town. All I think about is curling up next to you…making love to you."

"Stop reminding me." He groaned, and held her close. "No regrets about your career?"

She shook her head. "How could I? I'm doing a show in September, and starting up Soraya's Foundation is more than I ever hoped for." Her eyes filled. "But my most exciting career is going to be the role of your wife, and Corey's mother."

"I'm glad." He grew serious. "But with everything happening so fast, I seem to have forgotten one important detail." He reached into his pocket and drew out a velvet box.

"Oh, Holt," Leah gasped. "You didn't have to get me a ring."

"I want you and the whole world to know how much I love you," he told her. "You've given me something I never thought I'd find. Not just your love, but your acceptance and a sense of family. Because of that, I want to give you this." He opened the box, and a gorgeous round-cut diamond in an old-fashioned yellow-gold setting was nestled inside.

"Holt…" Leah gasped. "This is…breathtaking.

"It belonged to my grandmother. After she died my father had it put aside to give to me…for my wife one day." Holt gave Leah a half smile. "Dad would be happy that I'm marrying you. Zach told me how much he loved you, Leah. How much he loved your visits."

Leah realized how emotional this moment was for Holt. She couldn't speak as she blinked back tears.

"If you don't like it, I can get you something else."

"Don't you dare," she threatened. "This is the one I want. No other ring could mean so much. It's precious."

"No, you're the one who's precious," Holt told her as he removed the ring from the box and surprised her by going down on one knee. "Leah, I love you and can't imagine living my life without you. Will you marry me?"

"Oh, yes," she breathed and allowed him to slip the ring on her finger.

He stood and drew her into his arms. His head lowered and he placed a kiss on her mouth, but the tenderness soon grew intense. When he finally broke off, they were both fighting for air.

"You're not playing fair," she accused.

"Oh, but it feels so good." He brushed another kiss against her jaw and began working his way downward to her neck. "How about we forget the party and find someplace to be alone?" Holt asked, whispering other intentions against her ear.

Leah shivered. "Oh, Holt, I'd like nothing better," she said. "But we have family and guests arriving soon."

The sound of approaching footsteps alerted them that they weren't going to be alone for long. Her mother and father walked out onto the porch. "So this is where you are," Claire said.

With a grin, Holt stood behind Leah, gathering her against him. "Yes, and I've been trying to convince your daughter to run off with me."

"Be patient, son," Tim said. "Soon the party and wedding will be over and you can have Leah all to yourself." With a wicked grin, he pulled his wife into his arms and kissed her cheek.

The love between them warmed Leah's heart. There had never been any doubt that Tim and Claire Keenan loved each other.

Corey and Morgan came though the door. "Is anyone here, yet?" the boy asked his new parents.

"Not yet," Leah said.

Corey looked so handsome dressed in inky-black jeans and new boots. He had on a blue Western shirt and a bolo tie.

His earnest blue eyes looked from Leah to Holt. "Then can I talk to you first? It's important."

"Sure," Leah said as her parents and Morgan discreetly walked down the steps and toward the end of the driveway.

Corey appeared so serious. "Is it for sure that you're getting married?"

"Yes, it's for sure," Holt said, taking Leah's hand.

"And you really want me to live with you? Forever?"

Holt bit back a grin. "I think it's reasonable to say that you will live here until college, son. And the Silver R will always be your home." Holt crouched down to be on the same level with the boy. "What is it, Corey? You know you can ask us anything."

Corey glanced back and forth between the two of them. "I was just wondering if…since you're adopting me…if it would be all right to call you Dad and Mom right now, or do I have to wait until the judge says so?"

Leah's fingers tightened on Holt's shoulder. "No, you don't have to wait. We'd like that very much, son."

Holt hugged the boy. "We love you, Corey, and we'll always be here for you no matter what."

Leah ruffled her new son's hair. "I always wanted a little boy like you."

Corey stood back and struggled to hide the tears in the corners of his eyes. "And I'm going to be the best kid ever."

Leah and Holt laughed. "We just want you to be Corey."

"Okay," he said and ran down the driveway. "Grandma Claire, Grandpa Tim, they said yes." Leah's parents hugged the boy.

Holt sighed as he drew Leah into his arms. "What have we got ourselves into?"

She gazed up at the man she loved with all her heart. "I think we got ourselves a family. A loving family."

Holt's green eyes met hers. "Best day of my life was when I found you."

"I think the best day was when you decided to come to Destiny. When you decided to come home."

"We're both home." Holt's head lowered and covered Leah's mouth in another searing kiss.

There were more footsteps on the porch. "I hear there's going to be a wedding."

Leah broke away from her man and saw her sister Paige smiling at her.

"Paige," Leah called and ran into her arms. "You're home."

"Of course, I am. I wouldn't miss your special day."

Morgan joined them, and the three Keenan sisters hugged each other.

Like old times, they were together again.

n o c t u r n e ™

IT'S TIME TO DISCOVER THE RAINTREE TRILOGY...

There have always been those among us who are more than human...

Don't miss the dramatic first book by *New York Times* bestselling author

LINDA HOWARD

RAINTREE: *Inferno*

On sale May.

Raintree: Haunted by Linda Winstead Jones
Available June.

Raintree: Sanctuary by Beverly Barton
Available July.

SNLHIBC

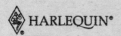

HARLEQUIN®

American ROMANCE®

A THREE-BOOK SERIES BY BELOVED AUTHOR

Judy Christenberry

Dallas Duets

What's behind the doors of
the Yellow Rose Lane apartments?
Love, Texas-style!

THE MARRYING KIND
May 2007

Jonathan Davis was many things—a millionaire,
a player, a catch. But he'd never be a husband.
For him, "marriage" equaled "mistake." Diane Black
was a forever kind of woman, a babies-and-minivan
kind of woman. But John was confident he could
date her and still avoid that trap.
Until he kissed her...

Also watch for:
DADDY NEXT DOOR
January 2007

MOMMY FOR A MINUTE
August 2007

Available wherever Harlequin books are sold.

www.eHarlequin.com   HARM07JC

HARLEQUIN®

///// NASCAR

In February…

Collect all 4 debut novels in the Harlequin NASCAR series.

SPEED DATING
by *USA TODAY* bestselling author
Nancy Warren

THUNDERSTRUCK
by Roxanne St. Claire

HEARTS UNDER CAUTION
by Gina Wilkins

DANGER ZONE
by Debra Webb

On sale February 2007

And in May don't miss…

Gabby, a gutsy female NASCAR driver, can't believe her mother is harping at her again. How many times does she have to say it? She's not going to help run the family's corporation. She's not shopping for a husband of the right pedigree. And there's no way she's giving up racing!

SPEED BUMPS *is one of four exciting Harlequin NASCAR books that will go on sale in May.*

SEE COUPON INSIDE.

///// NASCAR

SPEED BUMPS
Ken Casper

www.GetYourHeartRacing.com

REQUEST YOUR FREE BOOKS!
2 FREE NOVELS PLUS 2
FREE GIFTS!

HARLEQUIN ROMANCE®

From the Heart, For the Heart

YES! Please send me 2 FREE Harlequin Romance® novels and my 2 FREE gifts. After receiving them, if I don't wish to receive any more books, I can return the shipping statement marked "cancel." If I don't cancel, I will receive 4 brand-new novels every month and be billed just $3.57 per book in the U.S., or $4.05 per book in Canada, plus 25¢ shipping and handling per book and applicable taxes, if any*. That's a savings of over 15% off the cover price! I understand that accepting the 2 free books and gifts places me under no obligation to buy anything. I can always return a shipment and cancel at any time. Even if I never buy another book from Harlequin, the two free books and gifts are mine to keep forever.

114 HDN EEV7   314 HDN EEWK

Name	(PLEASE PRINT)
Address	Apt.
City	State/Prov. Zip/Postal Code
Signature (if under 18, a parent or guardian must sign)	

Mail to the **Harlequin Reader Service®**:
IN U.S.A.: P.O. Box 1867, Buffalo, NY 14240-1867
IN CANADA: P.O. Box 609, Fort Erie, Ontario L2A 5X3

Not valid to current Harlequin Romance subscribers.

Want to try two free books from another line?
Call 1-800-873-8635 or visit www.morefreebooks.com.

* Terms and prices subject to change without notice. NY residents add applicable sales tax. Canadian residents will be charged applicable provincial taxes and GST. This offer is limited to one order per household. All orders subject to approval. Credit or debit balances in a customer's account(s) may be offset by any other outstanding balance owed by or to the customer. Please allow 4 to 6 weeks for delivery.

Your Privacy: Harlequin is committed to protecting your privacy. Our Privacy Policy is available online at www.eHarlequin.com or upon request from the Reader Service. From time to time we make our lists of customers available to reputable firms who may have a product or service of interest to you. If you would prefer we not share your name and address, please check here. ☐

HARLEQUIN Romance.

Coming Next Month

#3949 THE SHERIFF'S PREGNANT WIFE Patricia Thayer
Rocky Mountain Brides
Surprise is an understatement for Sheriff Reed Larkin when he finds out his childhood sweetheart has returned home. After all these years Paige Keenan's smile can still make his heart ache. But what's the secret he can see in her whiskey-colored eyes?

#3950 THE PRINCE'S OUTBACK BRIDE Marion Lennox
Prince Max de Gautier travels to the Australian Outback in search of the heir to the throne. But Max finds a feisty woman who is fiercely protective of her adopted children. Although Pippa is wary of this dashing prince, she agrees to spend one month in his royal kingdom.

#3951 THE SECRET LIFE OF LADY GABRIELLA Liz Fielding
Lady Gabriella March is the perfect domestic goddess—but in truth she's simply Ellie March, who uses the beautiful mansion she is house-sitting to inspire her writing. The owner returns, and Ellie discovers that Dr. Benedict Faulkner is the opposite of the aging academic she'd imagined.

#3952 BACK TO MR & MRS Shirley Jump
Makeover Bride & Groom
Cade and Melanie were the high school prom king and queen. Twenty years on, Cade realizes that he let work take over and has lost the one person who lit up his world. Now he is determined to show Melanie he can be the husband she needs...and win back her heart.

#3953 MEMO: MARRY ME? Jennie Adams
Since her accident, and her problems with remembering things, working in an office can sometimes be hard for Lily Kellaway. But with the new boss, Zach Swift, it feels different. And not just because he is seriously gorgeous! Now he has asked her to join him on a business trip.

#3954 HIRED BY THE COWBOY Donna Alward
Western Weddings
Alexis Grayson has always looked after herself. So what if she is alone and pregnant? Gorgeous cowboy Connor Madsen seems determined to take care of her. And he needs something from her, too—a temporary wife! But soon Alexis realizes she wants to be a *real* wife to Connor.

HRCNM0407